The Secret of the Fiery Chamber

Danny Acero, the head of the raku pottery program at the East River Junction Crafts Festival, motioned for Nancy, Bess, and George to gather around him. "Raku can be a very safe process if you work calmly and in teams. That explains why everyone involved is wearing masks, gloves, long sleeves, and heavy hiking boots."

Danny's assistants hoisted up the kiln door, and Nancy gasped. The pots inside were so hot, they glowed like burning coals. Three potters skillfully unloaded the kiln, using long-handled cast-iron tongs. After the potters deposited the pieces into nearby containers, the hay and paper inside burst into flames and smoke billowed out.

Nancy's eyes began to water, but she blinked back the tears and angled herself upwind of the smoke so she could snap pictures of Bess and George helping Danny remove the lid from another container.

"Careful, you guys, you don't have protective masks or gloves!" Danny warned Bess and George as he lowered a pot into the open container.

But before Danny could put on the lid, flames, followed by a plume of oily black smoke, shot high in the air. Coughing and gagging on the noxious fumes, Bess stumbled back as sparks and embers showered down around her.

Nancy Drew
Mystery Stories

Available from MINSTREL Books

NANCY DREW® 159

THE SECRET OF THE FIERY CHAMBER

CAROLYN KEENE

A MINSTREL® BOOK

Published by POCKET BOOKS
New York   London   Toronto   Sydney   Singapore

This book is a work of fiction. Names, characters, places and incidents are products of the author's imagination or are used fictitiously. Any resemblance to actual events or locales or persons living or dead isentirely coincidental.

A MINSTREL PAPERBACK *Original*

 A Minstrel Book published by
POCKET BOOKS, a division of Simon & Schuster, Inc.
1230 Avenue of the Americas, New York, NY 10020

ISBN: 0-7434-0662-1

First Minstrel Books printing March 2001

10 9 8 7 6 5 4 3 2 1

Cover art by Franco Accornero

Printed in the U.S.A.

Contents

THE SECRET OF THE
FIERY CHAMBER

1

Sparks Fly

"Exactly who is this Theresa Kim?" George Fayne asked Nancy Drew one sultry Sunday afternoon in July. Nancy, George, and their friend Bess Marvin were standing beneath a blue-and-white banner welcoming visitors to the Third Annual East River Junction Crafts Festival.

"Whoever she is," Bess interrupted, "I'm glad Nancy decided it was worth the trip here to see her." Bess finished slathering sunblock on her shoulders and straightened the straps of her pink halter top. "I adore crafts fairs, and this one is supposed to be really special."

"All I know is that Dad got a call from a lawyer col-

1

league, John Kim, who said his daughter was here for the summer, and he left her e-mail address for me," Nancy said.

"So you e-mailed her we were coming today?" Bess asked.

"Actually, no," Nancy replied with a sheepish grin. "I thought it would be fun to walk up and surprise her. To see if we still recognize each other."

"Then you have met before," George said.

"Once, ages ago," Nancy explained. "Dad had some business with Mr. Kim and took me along to see him in Boston. I was about ten, and Theresa had just graduated from high school. She was too old for us to be friends. I did like her, though. She was already a pretty incredible artist and had won some big scholarship to study ceramics at a famous college in Upstate New York."

"Theresa must be pretty terrific," Bess said. "This place has a great rep in the crafts community. I can't believe it took me so long to check it out in person, considering we live only two hours away."

"Two long, *hot* hours, even in a convertible," George remarked, pushing back the red baseball cap that covered her short, dark curls.

Nancy smiled to herself. Sometimes she wondered how she could have two best friends who were as different from each other as fire and water. Though George and Bess were first cousins and the best of friends, they didn't look remotely related or even share interests. Fair-skinned, blue-eyed Bess had long, straw blond hair and a curvy figure, while dark-haired George was tall, slim, and athletic. Bess had an artistic streak, and her favorite sport was shopping; George's current passion was rock climbing.

Bess and Nancy wandered over to pick up maps at the information booth while George got a cold drink.

Nancy studied the map. Each exhibitor was listed alphabetically, with a number next to his or her name. The numbers corresponded to the booths in the layout. Nancy tucked a strand of her thick reddish blond hair behind an ear and surveyed the maze of vendor booths and tents, trying to orient herself.

"I'm impressed," Nancy told Bess. "Last time I saw East River Junction it was deserted."

"Not anymore!" a friendly voice said. Nancy turned to face the young woman who was standing behind the information counter. She wore a purple tank top beneath her overalls. Her name tag identified her as Andrea Washington, Woodworker. "Hi, I'm Andrea. And you're the first person I've met who was here before the Junction became a crafts village."

"I wouldn't call it 'being here,'" Nancy said, liking the forthright young woman instantly. "My dad and I just drove through on the way to someplace when I was still in elementary school. I can't believe how it's changed!"

3

Nancy took in the patchwork of farm fields. The festival had transformed the hilltop meadow they were standing in into a vast open-air market. The meadow sloped down gradually toward the East River, a ribbon of silver barely visible through a stand of trees along its bank.

"What was it like before?" Bess asked as George walked up.

"What was what like?" George wondered. "Did I miss something?"

"How East River Junction went from deserted to this," Andrea replied. "Simply put, some rich guy who had a thing for crafts left money in his will with instructions to buy the town and some of the surrounding farmland. Then he set up a foundation, to be run by the state arts council. Crafts artists and apprentices apply for grants to live and work here for up to two years. In exchange for studio space and rent-free housing, we have to give workshops and do exhibits. This festival's pretty major, and it makes up a good part of our year's business. You know, if you like demonstrations, the last part of the pottery raku demo will be starting soon. She pointed to a far corner of the festival grounds where a plume of black smoke rose lazily into the sultry air.

"I've never been to a raku ceramic firing, but I've always wanted to see one. Could we go before we look for Theresa?" Bess asked. Nancy and George nodded. Bess then glanced at her schedule and groaned. "Oh no, it started forty minutes ago."

"That's when the pottery was loaded into the kiln," Andrea explained. "It's due to come out now—that's the really exciting part."

The girls hurried across the field toward the raku demonstration, where grass had been cleared from a broad section of the field. At the edge of the grass, a couple of tables had been set up. One held a large jug of water and cups; the other was half covered with finished raku pots. Several beat-up lawn chairs were set up near the tables, but most of the onlookers had retreated down to the shade of the trees near the river or were hovering near the kiln, chatting with the potters.

Buckets of water and the last couple feet of a hose that ran up from the river ringed the perimeter of the firing area. Four metal trash cans were lined up a few feet from the small kiln; several more cans were standing on the grass. Thin trails of smoke drifted out from beneath the lids of the trash cans.

A wiry young man was peering into an opening in the side of the kiln. He wore a Chicago Cubs baseball cap backward, with a blue-and-white bandana under it. Welding goggles shielded his eyes, and thick suede gloves came halfway up his forearms.

"Almost ready!" he said, turning to the small crowd. "Make sure the cans are ready for the pots when we unload," he added, then spotted Nancy and her friends. He hung his goggles from the belt loops of his jeans and peeled off the gloves, revealing a tiny tattoo on his wrist.

"Hi!" He welcomed them with a quick smile. "I'm Danny Acero, and I'm in charge of the raku program here in the Junction. I've already given some background info, but I'll catch you guys up on things as we go along."

"Uh, great," Nancy replied. The guy was definitely in the hunk category. Only a couple of inches taller than Nancy, he had a lean, compact build. He was obviously used to working a crowd.

Danny motioned for everyone to gather around. "My assistants, Karen and Tom, will show you how to prepare the trash cans for the next step—the exciting part, when we take the pots out of the kiln.

"Just keep in mind," Danny went on, "raku can be a very safe process if you work calmly and in teams. Follow my—or Tom's or Karen's—directions exactly. If anyone gets excited and runs around, it can be very dangerous. So, designated helpers, make sure you wear the protective gear we give you. We're going to produce a lot of smoke and some serious fire in these cans!"

"That explains why everyone involved is wearing long sleeves and heavy hiking boots," Bess remarked. Like Nancy and George, Bess wore shorts, and she had plastic jelly sandals on her feet. "Guess that means we'll just watch this round."

"You can help set up," Karen said, having heard Bess.

George followed Tom to help cut open bales of hay, while Nancy and Bess helped Karen tear newspaper into small pieces, then put them into a big rubber barrel.

Danny glanced over at them and winked. "You guys are naturals, real team players," he said. "You know, we're starting a raku firing workshop on Wednesday. This demonstration is to whet your appetites."

"What if you haven't worked with clay?" Nancy asked.

"No problem," Danny told her. "We'll teach you how to form some simple pinch pots, which will look terrific after they're fired." Danny glanced around at the crowd. "Who knows what raku is?"

"A way to fire pots quickly," a small boy answered.

Danny laughed. "True—but that's not the whole story. Actually, raku is what we call a glaze-firing technique. Glazes are what give pots their finish. Glazed pots usually go into a cold kiln that's then heated slowly to a super-high temperature. Then it takes at least a day before the kiln is cool enough to open.

"But the fun of raku is that the firing all happens in forty minutes or so," Danny went on. "You put the glazed ware into a very hot kiln, then take it out while it's still almost molten and plunge it into either water or into a trash can to give it its special finish."

"Hey, Danny, they're ready!" Tom said from over by the kiln.

Karen handed out pairs of long suede gloves and bandanas to the helpers. "Okay, now tie one bandana over your hair and the other over your mouth bandit-style," Danny instructed them. "Teams of two will manage each barrel. As soon as I put a piece into the barrel, one member of the team will toss in burnable material: newspaper, hay, leaves. The other person will put the lid on *immediately.*"

As soon as the helpers all had their bandanas in place, Danny turned off the gas supply to the kiln. Tom and Karen hoisted up the kiln door, and Nancy gasped. The pots inside were so hot they glowed like burning coals. The three potters skillfully unloaded the kiln, using long-handled cast-iron tongs. After they deposited the pieces into the barrels, the hay and paper inside burst into flames and smoke billowed out.

Nancy's eyes began to water, but she blinked back the tears and angled herself upwind of the smoke so she could snap some pictures.

"Tom!" Danny cried suddenly as he lifted a particularly tall jug from the back of the kiln. "This piece needs its own barrel."

"None left," Tom told him.

"Wait!" Nancy cried. "What about the cans over here?"

"Grab one," Danny said. "Someone take off the lid and throw some burnable material in."

Nearest to the paper, George obeyed while Bess lifted the lid.

"Careful, you guys, you don't have the proper gear!" Danny warned as he hurried over to the barrel, carrying the heavy pot at arm's length. "Is there hay inside?" he asked.

"Plenty," Bess answered, peeking inside.

"Stand back," Danny ordered Bess. "Then put the lid on as soon as I dump this in the container."

Bess nodded, and Nancy lifted her camera to take Bess's picture.

Danny lowered the pot into the container. But before Bess could put on the lid, flames, followed by a plume of oily black smoke, shot high into the air. Coughing and gagging on the noxious fumes, Bess stumbled back as sparks and embers showered down around her.

2

The Fire's Gift

"Bess, stand still!" Nancy shouted, grabbing a shirt from the back of a lawn chair. She threw it on top of Bess's head to smother any sparks as Danny pulled Bess away from the fiery can.

Karen had quickly retrieved the lid and shoved it on top of the can.

"You okay?" Danny asked Bess, keeping an arm around her.

Bess gulped down water someone handed her. "I'm okay, it's just my hair . . ." She held out a long strand of her hair and wrinkled her nose. "It got singed. It smells awful!"she said ruefully.

"Everything smells awful," George said. "That smoke is really toxic."

"Yes, this particular smoke is really the worst," Danny admitted, turning to Bess. "You were lucky. Singed hair is almost normal during a raku firing, even with hats and bandanas. But what just happened here sure wasn't normal!"

His frown deepening, Danny approached the can. "Whatever fueled that little explosion has burned up by now." He motioned for Tom to take off the lid, then tossed a shovelful of sand into the container. "That'll smother the flames."

"So what happened?" Nancy asked as Danny leaned on his shovel and studied the can with a troubled gaze. "Whatever is in there smells like gasoline or oil."

"What you smell specifically is motor oil," Danny said, confirming her suspicions.

"In one of *our* reduction cans?" Tom remarked. "I sure didn't put any in."

"Except it's not one of *our* cans," Danny said. "Where did this come from, anyway?"

Karen cleared her throat. "I know," she said in a small voice. "I wanted to be sure we'd have enough containers, so I took it from behind the pottery shed today. Sorry. I didn't know there was oil in it. I just threw in some combustibles without looking inside."

"That can's probably left over from one of the staff firings. Someone who uses oil to get special effects," a woman said. At the sound of the deep southern accent, Nancy turned. The voice belonged to a slim, muscular woman with gray streaks running through her long, faded-blond ponytail. She seemed to be in her fifties and had a chiseled face with striking blue eyes. Nancy's glance drifted to her name tag, which read Ellie May Miller, Resident Artist, Ceramics Department.

Ellie May smiled at Karen. "You're new this summer, and part of being an apprentice is making mistakes. From now on, though, you should check any barrels before using them."

"Sorry, Ellie May," Karen apologized.

Ellie May patted Karen's shoulder. "Apology accepted, but now it's my turn to apologize. As head of the ceramics department I'm responsible for our guests. Did anyone get hurt here?"

"No," Danny said a bit nervously. "We were lucky. Just this girl—what was your name again?" he asked Bess.

"Bess, Bess Marvin," she said. "And I'm okay, really. Nothing a bit of a haircut won't fix," she joked.

"Ah, singed-hair syndrome!" Ellie May commiserated. "Well, we do owe you an apology. If this whole experience didn't scare you off, how about coming back Wednesday for our four-day raku workshop—including room and board—on the house?"

Bess's face lit up. "Free?"

12

Ellie May nodded.

Bess grinned excitedly. "I'd love it."

"If there's space in the workshop, maybe we'll come too," George said, turning to Nancy.

"It does seem like fun," Nancy said slowly, reading the workshop description over George's shoulder. "But four days—I don't know."

"Come on, Nan," Bess urged her. "You'll love it."

"Tell you what," Nancy said, seeing how important her coming to the workshop was to Bess. "Let me sleep on it. I'll decide by tomorrow. But both you and George should do it, with or without me."

"What if the workshop fills up?" Bess wondered.

Danny exchanged a quick glance with Ellie May. The director nodded. "Tell you what. No matter what, we'll fit in your friends. One of the houses has a three-person room in it. We'll assign you there, so there will be room for all of you."

"Not that anyone gets to sleep much around here," Tom joked.

After Ellie May left, the three girls decided they had had enough raku for the day and set off to find Theresa Kim.

"Theresa's booth is right there," Nancy said, pointing to a spot on the vendor map.

"Great, it's near Andrea's setup," George said. "Woodworking is so cool, and my dad's birthday is coming up. Maybe I can find something for him."

Nancy nodded as they strolled across the fair grounds, stopping to browse at various displays. "I've got my shopping list, too, though I'm not sure I'll find much within my budget. This work looks pretty expensive," she said.

"Prices are high here," Bess remarked, checking the price tag on a pair of earrings on a jeweler's table. "But the work seems better than at most of the other crafts fairs I've been to. I'm sure we'll find something affordable."

"Look!" George exclaimed, pointing toward the last row of vendors. "There's Andrea's table."

Andrea was wrapping a wooden salad bowl for a customer while several other people examined her wares. "Let's wait until her business has quieted down," Bess suggested as they approached. "The booth next to hers looks interesting!"

"More like the craftsman does," George teased under her breath. Bess gave her a playful shove and smoothed down her singed hair.

Nancy laughed, taking in the tall, auburn-haired guy sitting to one side of his booth. "Bess *does* have a point," Nancy admitted, deciding this guy was definitely worth looking at. As they approached the booth, Nancy's attention shifted from the guy's worn cowboy boots to his display. Shelves behind him held tall, elegantly designed pewter pitchers, candlesticks, and bowls. Arranged on a display table at the front of the booth were serving plates, small metal sculptures, and mirrors with beautifully tooled metal frames. "This work is beautiful," Nancy declared. "It could be in a museum."

"Meaning it's old-fashioned?" the craftsman asked archly.

Nancy bit her lip. "No, not old-fashioned. It's just that it reminds me of stuff I've seen in the museum back home."

"And where's that?" the guy asked, leaning forward in his chair. He took off his sunglasses and hooked them over the neck of his T-shirt.

"River Heights," Bess supplied before Nancy had a chance to answer.

The guy nodded. "Yeah, ever since that new crafts curator took over a few years ago, their metal collection has picked up. So I guess I should be flattered." He treated Nancy to a broad, open smile.

Nancy's eyes met his green ones. Nancy found him attractive but arrogant. The name on the tag on his shirt was Jonathan Walton. Still, as she examined a pair of salad servers, she decided he was good enough to afford a bit of an ego trip. Again, though, his prices were a bit beyond Nancy's budget.

"Are you looking for something in particular?" he asked, standing up. He was well over six feet and had muscular arms.

"Just browsing at this point," George answered,

picking up a metal letter opener and balancing it in her hand.

"Not me," Bess said, handing Jonathan a mirror she had been admiring. "Can't resist this!"

"Nice choice," he said, rewarding her with a smile. While Bess paid, Nancy asked Jonathan, "Do you know where Theresa Kim's booth is?"

"Ah, the famous TK. She hates it when I call her that," he added in a chummy tone that sounded pretty fake to Nancy.

"Sour grapes," Andrea said, leaning over from her booth. "She *is* famous, because she had some pottery in *Home and Design.* And the truth is, a lot of people here are a bit jealous of Theresa. Speaking as her roommate, I can tell you, though, she's an incredible potter *and* a terrific person."

"Whatever." Jonathan shrugged. "Anyway, she's over there." He waved down the row of booths.

Spectacular wasn't the word for Theresa's pots, Nancy realized as she and her friends stood in front of her booth a few minutes later. Nancy didn't know much about ceramics, but she could appreciate the simple elegance of Theresa's porcelain dinnerware and serving bowls. Her glazes were limited generally to a warm white or glossy black. Some of the larger bowls had tasteful gold-colored trim. Nancy could see why Theresa's spare, modern work had been featured in a top design magazine.

16

As the girls approached, the petite potter's back was to them. She was squatting in front of a carton, busily unwrapping dinner plates. Nancy winked at Bess and George, then put a finger to her lips and approached Theresa. "Excuse me, how much is that black bowl over there?" she asked.

Theresa straightened up and turned, following the direction of Nancy's finger. "Ninety-five," she answered with a smile, brushing a strand of thick, silky black hair off her face and tucking it back into her ponytail. She was only about five foot two and looked as if she barely weighed one hundred pounds. She wore a strappy T-shirt, and there was a scent of jasmine about her. Her complexion was flawless. Nancy remembered Theresa as a pretty girl, but she had blossomed into a beautiful young woman.

Nancy's eyes met hers, and she kept smiling. Theresa cocked her head, and slowly her face lit with recognition. "It's *you!*" she exclaimed after a beat. "Nancy Drew! Am I glad to see you!" she declared with a forcefulness that surprised Nancy.

"I wondered if you'd recognize me," Nancy laughed, her curiosity aroused. Her instincts told her Theresa hadn't tried to track her down because she was spending the summer near River Heights.

Theresa laughed a little self-consciously. "It did take a minute, though it shouldn't have." She giggled. "I guess we've both grown up." Then her dark eyes grew serious. "So are you just here by chance, or what?"

"I got your dad's message," Nancy said.

"But didn't he send you my e-mail address? When I didn't hear from you, I figured he forgot to tell your dad I wanted to get in touch."

"I thought I'd surprise you," Nancy admitted. "So instead of e-mailing, I came."

"Your work is awesome!" Bess said after Nancy had introduced her friends. She picked up a small white mug. She checked the price then asked Nancy, "Wouldn't this be a perfect gift for Hannah?"

"Who is Hannah?" Theresa asked.

"Hannah is our housekeeper," Nancy said. "I do love that mug, but actually, I was thinking of something more like this."

She pointed to a cup and saucer set, then said, "I could afford two sets of these, which would be nice for a gift."

Theresa made a face. "The one on display is my last one. "But I'll have more next week, and I could send both sets to you."

"But we'll be back next week," George said. "For the raku workshop."

Theresa nodded approval. "Great, so we'll be able to spend some time together. And my pots will be out of the kiln by Friday before the workshop's over."

"Except Nancy might bail," Bess said, butting Nancy's arm.

"But you have to come!" Theresa cried, visibly upset.

"I'd like to," Nancy said, wondering why it mattered to Theresa. "But four days—that's a lot. From what I saw today, one day of raku would suit me. Plus there's all that downtime between making the pots and then the firing Saturday."

"But there's so much to do here," Theresa told her. "Workshop participants are allowed to attend whatever demonstrations are going on in all the different crafts—woodworking, metals, fiber arts, bookbinding, papermaking—you name it."

Laughing, Nancy put her hands over her ears. "Stop, you guys! I'll think about it, and I'll let you know tomorrow," she promised Bess. "But in case I don't make it back," she said to Theresa, "I'm so glad we touched base."

Theresa gave Nancy's arm a squeeze. "I feel the same way, Nancy," she said, dropping her voice but keeping her hand on Nancy's arm. Nancy could feel that Theresa was trembling slightly. "My dad said you solve mysteries."

"Well, yes," Nancy admitted.

Theresa breathed a huge sigh. "You can't believe how glad I am to hear that." Dropping her voice even lower, she said, "I arrived here only three weeks ago, but I'm sure something really strange is going on. Strange and possibly illegal. You won't believe what I—"

"How could you do something like this?" a rude voice interrupted, and Theresa glanced behind Nancy and gasped.

3

The Blackened Tea Bowl

Nancy wheeled around. Danny Acero was bearing down on them, brandishing a small pot at Theresa. "Please, Theresa, don't stop talking because of me." Danny oozed sarcasm. "But first, tell me, is this your pot or what?"

Danny shoved the pot into Theresa's hand. It was sooty black and looked damp. Nancy caught a slight whiff of motor oil.

Theresa looked startled. "Where did you get this?" She was wearing white jeans and held the pot gingerly at arm's length.

"Do you admit it's yours?" Danny asked. "I found it when we dumped the ashes out of one of the raku trash cans—one with motor oil in it." Pointing to Nancy, he added, "She saw the whole thing, right?"

Nancy nodded cautiously. Why was Danny so mad?

Theresa wrinkled her nose. "Motor oil? Give me a break, Acero. I would never mess up one of my pots with motor oil." She put the pot aside. "I haven't done raku since school."

"So you say," Danny scoffed. "Cut the act, Theresa. This pot—of *yours*—has been raku fired."

"Looks that way, but I didn't fire it," Theresa defended herself. "You know raku isn't my thing."

"So you've said more than once. But obviously you've been doing a little raku on the side."

Theresa propped her hands on her slim hips and looked right up at Danny. "Look, no way I fired that pot. I've been here all day."

"It wasn't fired today," he pointed out, shaking his longish dark hair off his forehead.

"How do you know that?" Nancy asked, not liking Danny's attack on Theresa but curious in spite of herself.

"The pot was in the accumulation of ash at the bottom of that barrel, which was contaminated with motor oil from a previous firing."

Danny turned to Theresa. "You pretend to look down on raku and the kind of work I do, then when no one's looking you try your hand at it."

"That's crazy," Theresa told him. "I don't hate what you do, Danny. I like it, and I like raku. It just doesn't suit *my* work."

"Whatever," Danny snapped. "Just remember I'm in charge of raku here and the safety of the people involved. Next time you use a barrel, clean it out."

"I didn't use that barrel!" Theresa insisted, but Danny just threw up his hands and stormed away.

"What's his problem?" George wondered.

"Me," Theresa responded, clearly embarrassed and looking a little hurt. "He's jealous. He's got me pegged for being a snob because of where I went to school, and then that *Home and Design* spread came out."

"I didn't realize potters could be so competitive," Nancy mused.

"Generally people aren't, especially when they work in such different styles. Danny's is very organic, free-form, loose. It's really beautiful. I love it. Mine's what people call refined and more classical. Anyway, I guess he's really ticked off now." She pressed her palms to her temples, blew out her breath, then flashed a quick, tight smile at Nancy. "Customers," she said, heading back to the front of her booth. "I'll catch up with you later."

"Sure," Nancy replied. "And don't forget about the teacups," she said, grabbing a Post-it from a pad near Theresa's cash box. "Here's my e-mail address to let me know when they're done and if you still have some to spare."

Theresa smiled. "You'll get first dibs."

"And if you'd save these mugs for us," Bess added quickly, "we'll pay for them Wednesday when we come for the workshop."

"Thanks," Theresa said, running off to help a couple.

Nancy, Bess, and George ambled off to check out the rest of the show. As soon as they were out of Theresa's earshot, Bess remarked, "I didn't figure Danny for having such a temper."

"Me either," Nancy said as they stopped in front of a leather worker's display.

"More to the point, what was that *really* all about?" George wondered. "I think Danny heard something Theresa was starting to say to you. Maybe that's what sent him over the top, Nan."

Nancy frowned. "Theresa hadn't really said much, just that something strange was going on here. She was about to fill me in on what was bothering her when Danny interrupted."

"Yeah, he walked up ready for a fight," Bess observed.

"To put it mildly," George added.

"I've got the feeling there's some bad blood between him and Theresa," Nancy concluded. "Guess I had him figured wrong. I thought he was a pretty cool guy. But the way he treated Theresa just now was definitely uncool."

That night Carson Drew came into the study of the comfortable house he shared with Nancy and their housekeeper, Hannah Gruen, jangling his car keys. Nancy looked up from the computer and grinned at her dad. "Back from dinner out already?" she asked, swiveling around to face him.

Tossing his keys on the desk, Carson Drew returned her smile. "Actually it's pretty late."

Nancy glanced at the clock at the bottom of her computer screen and winced. "Must have lost track of time."

Her father peeked over Nancy's shoulder at the screen. "Good online sleuthing?"

"I've been checking out pottery web sites," she answered.

"So I take it your new interest in pottery has something to do with John Kim's daughter?" her dad asked, pleased.

"I looked her up and found her," Nancy said. She then told her father about the raku workshop. "And I found something to give Hannah for her birthday. Two lovely cups and saucers. They're just not ready yet."

"Speaking of Hannah," Nancy's father said, looking at his watch. "Can that really be the smell of her brownies in the kitchen?"

"Not just brownies, but super-spectacular brownies," Nancy responded.

"Now I'm glad I skipped dessert," her father said. "I'll grab a couple and check out the late news. There's a pretty heavy rainstorm headed this way. I hear it did some major damage west of here earlier today."

While her father made for the kitchen, Nancy scrolled down the screen until she hit a link for raku. A raku potter had thoughtfully written a brief history of the firing technique, which had originated in Japan in the late sixteenth century.

Contemporary American raku pots were displayed beside antique Japanese masterpieces. Nancy was intrigued by the photographs. The old Japanese pots were simple, hauntingly beautiful, yet even on a computer screen she could easily tell the difference between these rugged pots and the delicate, thin-walled work of Theresa's more classical pieces. Some of the American raku tea bowls were nearly indistinguishable from the Japanese originals. Others were wildly patterned or had bold, bright glazes.

The article explained that Japanese raku ware, both antique and contemporary, was highly prized and collectible, then gave the name of a ceramics auction site. Curious, Nancy surfed through the site and checked out the bulletin board, wondering if any of Danny's or Theresa's pots had turned up for auction, or if their names were mentioned.

The latest posting on the bulletin board caught Nancy's attention. It warned of counterfeit antique Japanese-style raku pots appearing on the market, through online as well as traditional auction houses. The posting suggested visitors check out buyers-beware.com for more detailed information.

With a click of her mouse, Nancy surfed to the new site. As she read through the web page, she was startled by the scope of what the writer called "this round of counterfeiting." Suggesting the existence of a whole counterfeiting ring, the site disclosed that not only were there numerous ceramic fakes, mainly masterful copies of important Asian pieces, but skillful, nearly perfect copies of Americana from the seventeenth century on. Descriptions and photos of pewter candlesticks and jugs, and handcrafted colonial furniture, including desks, chairs, tables, and lap desks, filled the web site.

Just then Nancy's computer beeped, signaling her that she had just received an e-mail message.

Nancy groaned. "Bess, I bet. Dying to know if I've decided to do that workshop." Nancy bookmarked the web page, then opened her message. She saw the sender's name and laughed. "Theresa!" She began to read the message.

Nancy—Sorry about the scene today at the festival. I do hope you decide to come to the raku workshop—and don't be put off by Danny. Whatever his problems are, they have to do with me. He's a great raku teacher and a lot of fun. It would be great to be able to visit with you during those four days. I'm teaching, but I have some free time, and we could hang out some. Oh, who am I fooling. Nancy, this isn't just a friendly invite. I really need your help. As I started to tell you earlier, I've come across something strange here. I'm not exactly sure what it means, though I have my suspicions. I was down by the river to take a quick swim one afternoon last week, when I discovered some shards. You won't

Suddenly the message ended. "Now what?" Nancy wondered, waiting a moment to see if Theresa's message would resume. When nothing happened, Nancy shot off a quick e-mail, asking what happened. She stayed online for a few more minutes, but Theresa didn't reply. It made no sense. Probably some computer glitch, Nancy thought. Frustrated, she heaved a sigh and started for the phone. Maybe Bess had a telephone number in the packet of information Ellie May had given her for the workshop.

"Hello?" Bess answered on the first ring.

"Did I wake you?" Nancy asked, suddenly realizing it was past eleven.

"No way, I've been checking out raku web sites," Bess said. "I am *sooo* excited about next week. Have you made up your mind?"

Nancy couldn't help but laugh at Bess's enthusiasm. "Not quite. But almost."

"Almost what?" Bess asked, in a pleading tone.

"Almost yes."

Bess cheered, but Nancy went on, "*Almost,* Bess, not definitely. Do you have Theresa's number at the village? If I do decide to go, I'll call first thing in the morning." Bess gave Nancy the number.

Nancy dialed.

The phone rang six times. Nancy winced. Maybe it was too late to be calling. On the seventh ring someone picked up the phone.

"Hello?" a woman answered in a voice thick with sleep.

"Theresa?" Nancy couldn't recognize the voice.

"Why—" The voice began, then Nancy heard a shrill, distant scream and the phone went dead.

4

Buyer Beware

The terrifying scream still reverberating in her ear, Nancy called into the phone, "Hello? Anyone there?" But the line was dead. Nancy jiggled the hook on the receiver, trying to revive the connection. It took several seconds before she got a dial tone. After punching Redial, she got a strange-sounding busy signal. Worried, she hung up and dialed the Junction number again but couldn't get through.

"You're still up?" her father asked from the study door.

"Yes," Nancy said, her face creased with worry. "I just called East River Junction to talk to Theresa, but the phone went dead. Now I can't get through."

Her father nodded. "That makes sense. I just heard that a severe thunderstorm was crossing that area. The power lines are probably down. I'm sure they'll have things up and running by morning."

"Power lines, of course." Nancy felt a surge of relief at the explanation, at least for the phones going dead, but why had Theresa cut off her e-mail so abruptly, and who in the world let out that scream?

Well, she'd find out in the morning when she'd try Theresa again. One thing was certain, Nancy was not going to miss that raku workshop. Theresa's hints of trouble intrigued her, and having an excuse to hang around the crafts village for a few days would be a good opportunity to investigate.

Wednesday morning Nancy, Bess, and George, armed with sleeping bags, approached the East River Junction crafts shop. The shop occupied a pretty but small white clapboard house with bursts of red and white petunias trailing out of sturdy ceramic pots that flanked the steps to the porch.

A sign was tacked to the porch railing: Registration: Raku, Tinsmithing, Papermaking, Photography. The line for registration trailed out of the store and onto the porch.

"Now, why didn't I expect a line," Bess moaned, stepping behind a gray-haired couple.

The woman in the couple turned around and

smiled warmly at Bess. "If you girls want, we'll watch your things, and you can visit the store. Everyone's been taking turns browsing inside."

"I'd like that," Nancy said, depositing her luggage at the foot of the steps. George and Bess followed suit. "We won't be long, but I wanted to ask about a friend who works here."

As they entered the store, George remarked, "I can't believe Theresa didn't return all those calls, Nancy. She must have figured you were worried. She doesn't even know we're coming."

"I e-mailed her again today, but she hasn't answered," Nancy said, approaching the sales desk.

"Are you looking for something in particular?" a round-faced girl with blond braids asked. She wore a name tag, which identified her as an apprentice in the instrument-making program, and her name as Melinda.

"Not exactly," Nancy answered, leaning against the glass-topped counter. "I'm looking for *someone*. Do you know Theresa Kim?"

Melinda's face brightened. "Sure. We have some of her work up front, though we can barely keep it in stock since that article appeared in *Home and Design*."

Nancy put up a hand to stop the girl. "I know that. I'm an old friend of hers, and I talked to her Sunday night, but the phone went dead. I've been trying to

call her since then, and I've left all sorts of messages. . . ." Nancy shrugged.

Melinda made a dismissive gesture with her hand.
"Not to worry. First of all, our phones were seriously
out from Sunday night until Monday morning. We
had a major storm—really scary. And then there's
that old message board problem. I rarely get my
messages, and half the time they're wrong. Besides,
Theresa's busy teaching an advanced workshop. I
haven't even seen her at dinner the past couple of
days."

Nancy felt disappointed. "Oh. I'd hoped to spend
time with her during the break in the raku workshop."

"You guys are taking that?" Melinda inquired,
twirling one of her braids.

"Yeah, if we ever get registered," Bess said, gestur-
ing toward the line.

Melinda looked sympathetic. "Actually, they've
called in more help. You'll be registered in no time.
And"—she turned to Nancy—"you'll be sure to run
into Theresa very soon."

A few minutes later the girls were registering.
Handing them each a map of the crafts village, the
young man at the desk said, "Orientation is in about
an hour, but since that's when raku is scheduled to
start, I'll get Melinda to give you a private tour now.
Hey, Mel!" he shouted, getting up from the table and
heading for the shop. "It's okay if you close shop for a

while. Would you please show these girls the layout of the village, on the way to their rooms?"

Melinda poked her head out of the door of the shop and replied, "Sure. Let me close up the cash register." A moment later she bounded down the steps and tossed the girls' bags in the back of an East River Junction pickup. "We'll leave the truck and your stuff here, and tour this end of the village first. Then I can drive your bags over to your residence, and you can follow in your car.

"As you probably know, this used to be a farm town—a hamlet really—with a general store, which is now our crafts shop, and a little post office. All the houses have been turned into residences, while many of the barns and outbuildings have become studios. Of course, some of the studios are totally new structures," Melinda explained as she started walking down the road.

Nancy stopped to admire the one stone building in the village. "What's that building?" Nancy asked.

"The administrator of the crafts village, Joe Bye, and his family live there, though he's out of town this week. Ellie May Miller, the pottery artist in residence, is in charge while he's gone. It's also our library."

"Can we check it out?" Bess asked.

Melinda nodded. "We can try. The library is officially closed until eleven. But I think I know where the key is, and, hey, when everyone else gets their village tour it's open. Why should you miss out on it?" she said, opening the heavy oak door of the building. Inside, the foyer was cool, with light filtering in through the stained-glass fan window over the entrance. The glass tinted the broad plank floor with puddles of red, gold, and blue.

"This place is awesome," George remarked as Melinda reached up to retrieve a key ring from a row of coat hooks by the door.

"It dates later than the rest of the village. The guy who built it was involved with the arts and crafts movement at the turn of the last century. That stained glass is genuine Tiffany." Mel led the way down a long hall. "The administrator's private quarters fill that side of the house, and, of course, the kitchen in the back. This," she said, stooping to open a door with her key, "is the library." The key turned freely in the lock. "Funny, it's already open."

The room, with windows facing east, was flooded with bright morning light. Coming in from the dimly lit hall, Nancy was momentarily blinded. She blinked and her vision cleared in time to see that someone was sitting at a table. He looked up.

"Danny!" Melinda said. "What are you doing here?"

"Checking something out," he answered casually. He closed the book he was reading and stood up. "So you guys decided to come back for raku?" He nodded. "Glad I didn't scare you away the other day."

He smiled at Nancy, and she realized he was trying to apologize for his behavior toward Theresa. She smiled back at him.

"You'll like it here, I'm sure," he said.

"So you'll lock up?" Melinda asked.

Danny shook his head. "I'll leave with you. I found what I needed," he said. "I'll just reshelve this book."

Nancy had started to follow the other girls to the door when she heard a loud thump. She turned to see Danny bending down to pick up the book from the floor. While he was bent over, she saw him deftly stash a sheaf of papers in the front of his shirt.

5

The Shadow Near the Shed

"Danny did what?" Bess stared at Nancy, her eyes round in disbelief.

"I'm sure I saw him steal something from the library," Nancy insisted as she zipped up her old faded jeans. The three friends were in their second-floor room, changing into old clothes before their first raku class. Overlooking a flowery meadow and a gray weathered barn, the room was quaint, with yellow floral wallpaper, ruffled curtains, and three twin beds. Bess had playfully taped each of the workshop name tags to the headboard of each bed.

George looked up from tying her sneakers, her face mirroring Bess's skepticism. "Nancy, why would he bother stealing anything? He's a resident here and free to use the library."

Nancy tugged a brush through her hair. "I know what I saw, and maybe there's a simple explanation for his stuffing papers inside his shirt."

"Like he didn't have a knapsack with him," Bess suggested.

Nancy asked herself if she was jumping to conclusions. Her gut instinct said no. "It's just something about that guy that bothers me," she admitted lamely.

As the girls closed the door to their room, they remembered there was no lock. All of the rooms had only old-fashioned metal latches.

Their residence, called Meadow House, was just a short walk down the blacktop to the pottery studios. The road sloped down slightly toward the river. The main studio was a long building, only a few years old but designed to fit in with the architecture of the village. It had a sloping roof, many windows, and a broad entrance, with barnlike double doors that stood open to the light breeze.

Through a window Nancy caught a glimpse of the back of Theresa's head. She was seated at a potter's wheel with her back to the door. Students were gathered around her, and she looked engrossed in her job. Nancy knew she'd have to wait for lunch to talk to her.

Several outbuildings flanked the pottery studio. An open-sided shed stood on the side of the building farthest from the river and the trees. A brick chimney rose from the top of its tin roof. Sheltered by the roof, a large brick kiln stood on the concrete floor. The arched door of the kiln was open. As they drew near, Nancy could see it was empty, and the bricks lining the interior were lustrous and shiny.

Danny was standing in front of the kiln, talking to a few workshop participants. The rest of the class was gathered around a card table set up on the grass beneath the shade of some trees, talking to Danny's assistant, Tom. Three long tables also hugged the shade of the trees and the overhang of the pottery studio roof. A few potter's wheels had been moved into the yard, and a couple of women wearing workshop name tags were already at the wheels. Nancy, Bess, and George headed for the group at the card table.

"Ah, here they are, our last three stragglers," Tom said with a welcoming grin. After asking them about their previous experience with clay, Tom assigned them to an appropriate group: Nancy and George found themselves at the novice table, while Bess joined the intermediate students. Danny started out with the novices, while Tom and Karen attended to the other students.

Danny pulled an old barrel up to the head of the table and straddled it. After they had all introduced themselves, he put the book at one end of the table. Little yellow Post-its flagged some of the pages. "You all might want to check out this book while we pass around workshop handouts. There are some wonderful examples of ancient Japanese tea bowls—mugs without handles," he explained. "You're going to concentrate on making small tea bowls for this workshop." He tapped the stack of handouts on the table to straighten them out. "Everybody please take a set of these handouts. I copied material from sources in the library. Most of it is just general information, and for you beginners, the glaze recipes on the last two pages probably won't be much use to you unless you continue working with clay."

Grinning, Danny continued, "Don't let all the technical info scare you off. But do read the historical background."

As the handouts reached Nancy and George, George took one and nudged Nancy's knee under the table. "See, that's all he was doing," she whispered. "Pulling together this stuff."

"Probably," Nancy admitted softly. But if George was right, why would Danny try to hide the papers in his shirt?

Before Nancy could give it another thought, Danny passed out balls of clay and demonstrated how to make simple pots by pinching out the ball of clay into a round tea bowl. He went around and helped the students get started, then left to talk to the intermediate and advanced groups.

Nancy was surprised at how quickly she got the hang of forming little pots. The process of pinching the clay took a lot of concentration, but it had a calming effect, and took Nancy's mind off Danny. By lunch break she had finished three small tea bowls— all fairly even, and to her eye actually attractive.

"Isn't this great?" Bess enthused as the three girls headed back up the road toward the farmhouse in which the dining area and communal kitchens were located. "I learned how to make some really cool-looking plates and tiles. Tell me, don't you just love all this?"

George readily agreed as they sauntered up the road. "I've already read some of Danny's material, and it is really amazing to learn how the high temperature of a kiln transforms the clay from basically mud to something that could last forever."

"What's wrong?" Bess asked as she noticed Nancy poking around in her bag.

"It's no big deal," Nancy replied. "I left my sunglasses in our room. I'll run over to Meadow House and get them and catch up with you in a few minutes."

Nancy doubled back to Meadow House. She jogged up the stairs and pushed open the door to her room. There was a faint whiff of jasmine in the air. Nancy sniffed, trying to remember where she'd smelled it recently. Before she could recall, she noticed a note pinned to her pillow.

She opened it and read aloud to herself, " 'Sorry I

couldn't talk to you this morning during the workshop, but there were too many people around. Meet me tonight during the after-dinner bonfire. I'll be behind the pottery studio, near the woodshed. Come alone. Don't let anyone see you. Thanks, T.' "

"T—" Nancy murmured, and then nodded. The scent of jasmine. Theresa had been wearing jasmine perfume on Sunday. The note was from Theresa, of course. And, of course, Nancy wouldn't miss meeting her tonight for the world, if for no other reason than to find out why she was acting so mysterious.

Hugging the shadows that evening, Nancy crept along the side of the pottery studio, her head bent low. From behind her she could hear the voices of the crowd gathered around the bonfire. Melinda and one of the other apprentices had pulled out guitars and were leading the group in a round of well-known folk songs. It was with some reluctance that Nancy had slipped away from the campfire. As she rounded the corner of the pottery studio, she studied the layout of the nearby sheds.

"Theresa?" she called softly, carefully peeking in through a back window. The studio seemed empty. An uncovered mound of white clay sat on a potter's wheel just to the left of the window. A towel and apron were thrown over the seat of a chair in front of the wheel. Three unglazed bowls, their white clay

42

still gleaming with moisture, were on a table next to the wheel. Whoever had been working inside obviously intended to return quickly. Nancy ducked away from the window, trying to distinguish the various shadowy outbuildings and sheds. "Theresa?" she called again, a little louder.

"Nancy?" Theresa responded softly, then joined Nancy beside the studio building. "I'm so glad you came."

"Is anyone in there?" Nancy asked, indicating the studio.

Theresa shook her head. "I was. I had to get working on an order I took at the festival. Everyone else is at the bonfire—the weekly Wednesday ritual. It's part of Ellie May's rah-rah scene," Theresa added, a faint edge to her voice.

"So what's happening, Theresa?" Nancy asked. "Why didn't you finish your e-mail to me the other night—the way it broke off midsentence was really weird."

"Sorry. But my roommate walked in and I didn't want her—or anyone—to see what I was about to write," Theresa said apologetically.

"But you never returned my calls, either. I was getting worried. Did you get my messages?"

Theresa held up one finger. "Message—singular." She shook her head. "Messages seem to disappear from the bulletin board. But I didn't return the one call because I've been swamped. Also, problems with the computer-operated kilns cropped up the next day because of that big storm Sunday."

Nancy nodded. "Yes. I heard about it. In fact, when I phoned you after you cut off your e-mail someone answered the phone, but then it went dead." Then Nancy remembered the scream, but before she could ask about it, Theresa drew her closer.

"Nancy, I don't want to get interrupted again. Why I needed to talk to you was this." Theresa took Nancy's hand and dropped in it what felt like a small bowl. "Careful, the edges are sharp. I didn't want to file them in case I found more pieces, and in case they're evidence."

"Evidence?" Crouching close to the ground, Nancy held the bowl in the patch of light from the window. It was a beautifully shaped, heavy-walled pottery tea bowl—more like half a tea bowl. The outside had a pale glaze, though Nancy couldn't make out the exact color in the dim light. Several dark strokes of paint or glaze decorated one side of the bowl. To Nancy the paint strokes looked like some sort of Japanese or Chinese writing. "Evidence of what, Theresa?"

Theresa didn't answer directly. Hunkering down next to Nancy, she propped her elbows on her knees. "I went for a swim in the river about ten days ago to get away from, well, the scene here."

44

Nancy tried to read Theresa's face in the dark. From the few hints Theresa had just dropped, plus Jonathan's and Danny's jealous reactions to her, Nancy was pretty sure Theresa was having a hard time socially in the village.

Theresa sighed, then went on in a more businesslike tone. "I came across a pile of pottery shards, where the weeds are thick along the riverbank. I guess I was curious about how they got there, since it's a good half-mile walk from the studios. So I tied them in my towel and took them back to the village. That night I washed them off and was pretty shocked by what I'd found. Check out the cracks in the glaze surface, and the way it looks very worn." Theresa ran her finger down the pot's surface, tracing a fine web of lines. "I couldn't believe it. This looks like a very valuable seventeenth-century raku pot."

"That old?" With awe, Nancy fingered the pot fragment in her hand. "Here? How?"

"My thoughts exactly. It didn't make sense. So I glued them together carefully. Don't look worried— I used a special glue that can be dissolved with the proper solvent and won't injure the shards."

"Who would throw something like this in the river?"

"No one, intentionally. Not if it's the real thing," Theresa said. "Sometimes pieces turn up and no one alive knows how valuable they are. There *is* that possibility . . ." Theresa's voice trailed off.

"I hear a big *but* in your voice," Nancy said, sitting back on her heels.

Theresa smiled wanly. "A very big *but,* Nancy. I'm now sure the pot is a fake. A counterfeit raku piece—a masterful copy, but still a copy. I'm *almost* sure of that!"

Nancy eyeballed the pot again, then told Theresa about her investigations on the Internet.

"I've heard about that," Theresa told her. "And the problem is even bigger than just raku pots. All types of Asian ceramics—Korean, Chinese, Japanese—are being counterfeited, and beautifully, I might add. It takes a real expert to tell the difference between the fakes and the real thing."

"What in the world motivates someone who can make such a good fake to turn to counterfeiting?" Nancy wondered.

"Money, what else?" Theresa answered.

"It just seems like cheating yourself," Nancy said. "As well as all the people who pay incredible money for fakes."

"This is a serious problem, and it is considered a major crime," Theresa said. "It's fraud, and who-ever's doing this can be facing serious jail time."

Nancy cautiously asked, "Do you have any idea who *could* be doing it?"

Slowly Theresa nodded. "Yeah, I have my suspi-cions. Danny could have made this raku piece. He's pretty good at Chinese and Japanese calligraphy, like the kind used here. But he couldn't possibly pull off the other ceramic fakes featured online. They are too refined—more than one potter must be involved, and I have a good idea who—"

A movement at the corner of her eye made Nancy look up. She clamped a hand over Theresa's mouth and pointed behind the potter. Light pouring out of the studio's side windows cast a skinny shadow against the wall of a shed. Nancy couldn't tell if it belonged to a man or a woman. She signaled for Theresa to keep quiet.

Half holding her breath, Nancy crept beneath the back window of the studio before straightening up. Motioning again for Theresa to freeze, she edged toward the corner of the building. Bracing herself with one hand against the clapboards, she peered around the side in time to see a lanky figure melt into the shadows between a woodpile and the kiln shed.

6

Danny to the Rescue

The shadowy figure ducked behind the woodpile, then emerged a second later on the far side of one of the sheds, only to disappear again in the maze of out-buildings. Nancy set off after the eavesdropper. She couldn't tell if the person was male or female, only that whoever it was didn't seem to be aware of her.

Good break for me! she thought as she cautiously picked her way across the yard, hoping not to trip over any of the bales of hay or buckets littering the ground. Moving silently, she neared the tight cluster of sheds. The eavesdropper couldn't have gone far. Nancy reached into her pocket and felt for the pen-light she always carried with her. If she could catch the prowler unaware, she might be able to identify him with the help of her light.

"Nancy! Are you okay?" Theresa's sudden shout made Nancy spin around. Ignoring Nancy's instructions, Theresa was hurrying toward her, a flashlight in her hand, the broad beam bobbing as she approached.

Frustrated, Nancy shook her head. "Yes, but I've probably lost him now."

"Him?" Theresa grabbed Nancy's arm. "So it was a guy you saw?"

"I couldn't tell. Whoever it was is probably gone now."

"I guess I scared him off," Theresa said contritely. "Sorry, I was afraid something had happened to you."

"Not to worry," Nancy tried to assure her. Then they headed back toward the studio. As they neared the door, Nancy glimpsed two people inside putting on work aprons. She stopped just short of the building and asked Theresa, "Have you mentioned your suspicions about Danny to anyone else?"

"No way!" Theresa said. "There's not enough proof. And I'm not sure that what I found *is* a fake. The only way to be sure is to have an expert check it out."

"Would someone at the village be expert enough?" Nancy asked.

"Here?" Theresa was aghast. "As I said, I'm not sure who's caught up in this scam—if it is a scam. I'm afraid to trust anyone here. I mean, what if it's *not*

Danny?" Theresa paced away, chafing her arms. "Anyway, that's why I contacted you. Nancy, I read something recently about a museum in River Heights. Is there an Asian studies person on staff there?"

"I don't know," Nancy told her. "But my dad would know. Actually, I can get away tomorrow. We have a morning break."

"That's right."

"I'll call my dad tonight. If he knows of any Asian art expert, and if she or he isn't more than a few hours away, I'll take the pot to be checked out. With any luck I'll be back tomorrow in time for Andrea's woodworking demo—I don't want to miss that."

"Yeah, she'd like that," Theresa agreed. "Meanwhile, tomorrow I'll see if I can turn up more shards."

The next morning Nancy hurried down to the administrative wing of the River Heights museum, looking for the office of the Ceramics Department curator. A quick phone call to her dad the night before had proved fruitful. Not only did he know the curator, Ron Darien, but he volunteered to phone Mr. Darien first thing. Nancy's father ended by warning Nancy to be careful, as art fraud sometimes involved pretty unsavory characters.

The character who looked up from his desk as Nancy poked her head in the small office was anything but unsavory. He was a short, round-faced, middle-aged man wearing a cheerful, boldly printed tie. At the sight of Nancy he jumped up and greeted her with great warmth. "You must be Nancy, Carson Drew's daughter. Come in, come in!" Ron Darien waved Nancy toward his desk, then quickly removed a pile of papers from a chair before scooting it in her direction.

Nancy pumped his hand, sat down, and looked around while he poured her a cup of tea. Every surface of the small office was heaped with papers, file folders, and printouts. But tucked amid the clutter were pieces of exquisite Asian art. "I don't know how to thank you for seeing me on such short notice," Nancy told him, taking the small broken tea bowl from his hand. It was simple and modern, and resembled Theresa's work.

"I figured if Carson said it was important, then I'd better hear you out," Mr. Darien said.

"So Dad didn't fill you in on anything?" Nancy asked.

Ron shook his head. "He said you'd tell me what's happening. So . . . ?" he prompted her, leaning back in his chair.

Nancy carefully set down her tea and took the tea bowl fragment out of her bag. Mr. Darien leaned forward to watch as she undid the layers of bubble wrap and tissue paper. "This," she said, setting the mended tea bowl directly in front of him.

The curator's face registered surprise, then concern. "Where did you get this?"

Nancy told him about Theresa's finding the shards. "I hope it's no problem that she put them together . . ."

"Problem? This woman has the makings of a very good conservator. No one on my staff here, or at the last museum I worked at in Kansas City, could have done a better job."

"So is it as old as it looks?"

Before responding, Mr. Darien took a magnifying glass out of his top desk drawer and carefully examined the pot, paying particular attention to the broken edges. Putting it down, he regarded Nancy with a frown. "I think it's a fake. In fact I'm almost sure, though I'd have to do a couple of tests on it to find out. I'm about ninety-nine percent certain that this is not ancient clay."

"Does it look like old clay from Japan?" Nancy asked.

"Oh, yes. It's been very cleverly formulated. But clay bodies mined in Japan have a different proportion of certain minerals from those mined here."

"So someone could have added materials to this clay to make it look like the real thing," Nancy surmised.

"Yes, someone very smart, with a lot of expertise and knowledge. And whoever's behind this is playing for high stakes, Nancy. Fakes like this aren't made for casual collectors but for the serious art market."

Nancy thought a moment, then asked, "How does this kind of scam work?"

"Generally, the most highly skilled artisans and artists are approached by unscrupulous antique dealers and auctioneers to create fakes. The pay is high enough to tempt many honest craftspeople."

"But if they get caught it must wreck their careers—as well as land them in jail."

"Ah, but catching people is very hard. This piece, for example, could have been made anywhere. It's good to know where it was found."

"But that's only the first step in trying to find the counterfeiter," Nancy said thoughtfully. "So what's next?"

"If you'll let me have the pot for now, I'll have it examined more closely. Then if it's a fake, I'll call in the authorities. It's crucial to try to get to the root of this."

Nancy checked her watch, then pushed back her chair. "Theresa is keeping her eye out for more shards, and of course, I'll let you know if anything turns up."

Ron Darien got up, heaving a sigh. He studied Nancy. "Your father told me that you were capable of handling whatever comes up, but, Nancy, if this pot does lead you to the source of the fakes, be careful. These people can be dangerous."

"I know that," Nancy assured him.

After leaving Mr. Darien, Nancy grabbed a sandwich and soda from a food cart outside the museum and headed straight back to East River Junction. Traffic was light, and Nancy pulled off the main road and onto the smaller blacktop leading to the Junction in plenty of time to catch Andrea's woodworking demonstration.

She went through the open gates to the village, then made a left past the village shop and the curator's cottage and headed down toward Meadow House. She'd worn a skirt and heels to her meeting with Mr. Darien and needed to change her clothes. With any luck she'd be able to snatch a private moment with Theresa to catch her up on her meeting with Mr. Darien. Suddenly the shrill wail of a siren broke into her thoughts.

Checking her rearview mirror, Nancy caught her breath. A fire engine was bearing down on her at high speed. Nancy pulled over to the shoulder, letting the engine roar past, two police cars in its wake. She looked ahead past the flashing lights, and her mouth went dry. Smoke was pouring out of the basement of a large farmhouse—the house where Theresa lived.

7

Smoke Screen

Nancy swerved back onto the road and sped toward the residence. She pulled in behind one of the police cars and jumped out, slamming the door behind her. Nasty plumes of dark smoke shot out of the basement windows, but the rest of the building seemed okay.

"Danny's in there!" Bess cried, rushing up and gripping Nancy's arm. Bess steered her through the small crowd milling outside the building. The old-fashioned hatch doors to the basement were open, and several firefighters were standing on the steps aiming hoses at the blaze. Bess gestured wildly toward the upper floors of the house. "He ran in there just when the fire trucks came. He wanted to rescue some quilts or something from inside."

Bess and Nancy worked their way toward George, who was standing right at the edge of a police barricade. "Where's Theresa?" Nancy asked, quickly scanning the crowd.

"Inside," George said grimly. "Lots of people were in the building, though most have gotten out already. Theresa stopped back here with Andrea to help her carry materials over for her demo later."

Nancy cast a worried glance upward. "Isn't their room on the top floor?"

George nodded as two other firefighters came down the front steps of the building, guiding Theresa and Andrea. "Oh, here they come. They're all right!" Bess cried with relief.

"There's Danny, too," Nancy noted as the dark-haired potter emerged, coughing, from a side door. He was wearing his knapsack on his back and carrying a large wicker basket. He lifted the basket toward the crowd, holding it to display one of the folded quilts inside. A cheer went up from the onlookers, followed by a round of applause.

"Are you crazy?" one of the firefighters yelled at Danny, obviously not impressed by his act of heroism. "You could have been killed in there if the fire had gotten out of control."

"But I wasn't," Danny said, shrugging off the man's concerns.

"More to the point, someone else—like one of my men—could have been hurt trying to save you," the fire chief broke in.

Danny's jaunty expression faded. "Hey, man, I didn't think of that."

"Well, you should have," the fire chief added. Then he turned to address the crowd. "The fire seems to have been confined to the basement and is out now. As soon as we're sure everything's okay, you can go back in."

"What started the fire?" Nancy wondered.

One of the officers nearby overheard her. "The chief says the fire probably started with a pile of papers and rags in the basement."

"Who's in charge around here?" the fire chief asked.

Ellie May stepped up from the fringe of the crowd. "I am—at least for this week," she said, introducing herself. "Was the fire suspicious? Is there anything I need to do now?"

The chief answered, "We can't rule out arson so quickly, but most likely the fire was not intentionally set. Those rags and papers in the basement were stacked too close to the heating elements of the water heater."

Ellie May frowned. "What rags and newspapers?"

"Oh no!" Melinda gasped. "From that papermaking workshop earlier this month. We had to move the workshop into the kitchen of the residence. Someone must have put the leftover materials in the basement when they cleaned up."

Ellie May pursed her lips. Turning toward the fire chief, she said tightly, "I can't imagine how this happened, but I assure you I'll run a tighter ship."

The fire chief looked appeased. "I'm issuing you a warning. Our fire inspection team will be checking the whole village, and if we find any more violations, you could be closed to the public until everything meets our fire code."

"Of course, of course," Ellie May said, sounding nervous.

Theresa touched Nancy's arm. "I'm going back upstairs to help Andrea haul stuff out of the room."

"Need help?" Nancy volunteered, hoping for a chance to get Theresa alone.

Theresa nodded, then with a furtive look around added, "Did you see the curator at the museum?"

Nancy nodded, but just then Andrea walked up with Bess and George. "George said you'd help haul my gear over to woodworking in your car."

"Glad to help," Nancy said, then exchanged a quick glance with Theresa. Filling her in on the details of her visit with Mr. Darien would have to wait until later.

Inside, the house smelled only slightly smoky.

"This'll only take a minute," Andrea assured them,

opening the door to her third-floor room. The room was spacious and airy but somewhat cluttered. As in most old farmhouses, there were no closets, but near the foot of each bed was a tall oak wardrobe.

Andrea walked over to the open wardrobe. She poked her head in and let out a horrified cry. "I don't believe this! It's gone!" She turned, ashen faced, toward the other girls.

"What's gone?" Bess asked.

"My lap desk!"

Theresa gasped. "No way! It was there before the fire. You'd started pulling it out of the bottom of the wardrobe when your mom rang you on the cell phone. Then the fire started."

"What's a lap desk?" George asked, stooping to check the bottom of the wardrobe. "Like, how big is it?"

"It's small, not much bigger than Theresa's laptop. It was a traveling desk, probably made for a lady, dating from about 1800," Andrea said, her voice trembling. "It's really valuable, plus it's sentimental. It's been in my family for ages. It's what made me decide to become a woodworker." Her words dissolved into tears.

Putting a soothing hand on Andrea's back, Nancy asked gently, "And you're sure you didn't pack it before the fire?" Nancy motioned toward two duffel bags on Andrea's bed. "Could you have put it in one of those and just forgotten in all the commotion?"

"No. I'd remember!" Andrea insisted, but she grabbed each duffel, unzipped it, and displayed the contents.

Nancy thought quickly. "The police are still downstairs," she said. "Let's hurry and report this."

The girls rushed outside. The fire truck was heading back up the road, followed by one patrol car. The second set of officers were climbing into their car when Nancy ran up. "Officers," she called, "there's been a burglary."

The officer on the passenger side got out and grabbed his notebook. "Slow down. Now, what happened, and when?"

"During the fire, I'm sure of it, someone walked off with my lap desk," Andrea said, wiping the tears from her face. Bess handed her some tissues. While Andrea blew her nose, the officer cleared his throat.

"I know there was a lot of commotion, but I'm sure I would have noticed someone walking out of the house with a desk."

Nancy checked out the man's name tag. "Officer Martinez," she said, "this desk was small. The size of a laptop computer, maybe a little bigger," she added quickly, checking with Andrea. "It was old and very valuable, and maybe stealing it was motive enough to start a fire."

The officer studied Nancy. "It was *that* portable?"

Theresa and Andrea nodded.

The officer took the information, as well as Andrea's cell phone number. "You should start locking your doors if there's a burglar at work," he suggested as he climbed back into the car.

"There are no locks," Theresa informed him.

As they filed back into the house, Nancy asked Andrea, "If the desk is so valuable, why did you bring it here, knowing how little security there is?"

"For demonstrations," Andrea explained. "Students learn how to make templates from original antique pieces. They learn what forms of joinery were used in any particular period, what kinds of woods or varnishes—everything they need to know to understand good craftsmanship."

"So I guess when they finish, the better students can make pretty good fakes," Nancy suggested with a light laugh.

Andrea frowned. "No way. It'd take years to master the craft well enough for that, and even then"—she shrugged—"there are too many variables to pull off a copy good enough to fool experts."

Nancy's curiosity was piqued. So Andrea actually taught old methods of fabricating items. Hadn't buyerbeware.com mentioned counterfeit colonial wooden items as well as fake Asian ceramics turning up at auctions?

George broke into Nancy's thoughts. "So this sure

cramps your style for your demo today. What will you do?" she asked Andrea.

Andrea stopped and shook her head, dismayed. "I don't know. I hadn't even begun to think about that problem."

Theresa gave her a hug. "I'm sure we'll come up with—" Suddenly she broke off and brightened. "I know. Isn't there a colonial highboy chest in the curator's cottage?"

Comprehension dawned on Andrea's face. "Of course! I can use that and just shift my demo more to the methods of joinery. And maybe we can get some guys to help us move it to the woodworking studio. Now, where are all those guys when you need them?" she exclaimed.

"At your service—I think," Jonathan Walton boomed, striding toward the group on the stairs. Without his baseball cap and with his longish hair in a ponytail, Jonathan looked even hunkier and more attractive to Nancy than on Sunday, when she had first met the metalworker.

He stopped to sniff the air; it was still acrid with smoke. "What's that awful smell? Tell me it's not dinner." He staggered back comically, then swept a thick lock of auburn hair off his face.

"Where have you been? Didn't you know there was a fire?" Andrea told him.

"Fire? Here?" He looked stunned.

"How'd you miss it?" Bess wondered, angling herself so she could look right up into Jonathan's intense green eyes.

Nancy smothered a smile. Even in a crisis Bess would never forgo a chance to flirt.

"Guess I was too busy working in my studio to check out the noise. Though," he said, scratching his head and looking thoughtful, "I do recall hearing sirens. I thought they were out by the main road."

"Oh my gosh!" Theresa gasped. "Jonathan, you should check your room. Andrea's lap desk was stolen during the fire. You should be sure nothing of yours is missing. Don't you have some really nice old pewter pieces up there?"

Jonathan whistled softly, then bolted up the steps. "You bet I do," he shouted back over his shoulder. The girls hurried upstairs after him. By the time they reached the top floor Jonathan had already emerged from his room. It was a corner room, next to Theresa and Andrea's. The door was open. Nancy noticed it was on the small side and had a single bed.

"Nope, nothing's gone missing," Jonathan said. He was holding a nicely shaped pewter pitcher in one hand and a candlestick in the other. "Guess the thief wasn't into metal."

"Or didn't know you had those," Nancy pointed out as George and Bess followed Theresa and Andrea back into their room. George hefted up the heavier duffel bag and carried it into the hall.

"Nancy!" Theresa's cry made Nancy turn around. Theresa stood in front of her desk, a look of shock on her face. "This is crazy," she gasped. "My sketchbook! Someone stole that, too!"

8

Faking It

"No way!" Andrea gasped. "Your sketchbook was on your desk. I just saw it."

"Just?" Nancy echoed, hurrying over to the desk, where Theresa was staring dumbfounded at the clutter next to her laptop. "Andrea, what do you mean by 'just'?"

"Just, as in before we went downstairs."

"Now or before the fire?" George inquired, starting to look around the room.

Andrea pressed her hands to her temples. "I don't know. I thought I saw it when we came back up to the room after the fire. I can't swear I did, though," she added lamely.

"Pretty likely the same person who ripped off Andrea's lap desk made off with the sketchbook," Jonathan commented from the doorway. He seemed intrigued but not particularly troubled. With a shrug he added, "Good luck looking, though I can't imagine why someone who'd be savvy enough to take a valuable colonial lap desk would bother with a bunch of notes and doodles."

"Doodles?" Theresa's head shot up, and she glared at Jonathan. "I didn't doodle in that book. I used it to do detailed sketches of my latest design ideas. And in the back was a list of customers and orders that I'd taken during the festival. I haven't had time to enter them into my computer. How am I ever going to reconstruct those orders or that customer list?"

"It's not the end of the world," Jonathan remarked coolly.

Theresa didn't grace that remark with a response. She got up, turned her back on Jonathan, and began opening and closing dresser drawers.

"Let's search the room thoroughly. Maybe in the commotion of the fire, you forgot where it was. Try to retrace your steps," Nancy advised. "Maybe you left it back in the pottery studio."

"No. No, I'm sure I didn't," Theresa insisted. "I know I brought it back here last night. I was sketching some new ideas just this morning right after I got up."

"Did you check your bag? Would it fit in there?"

Nancy asked, pointing to the black messenger-type shoulder bag hanging from a hook.

Theresa jumped up to check the bag. "It's not here," she said glumly.

The girls searched thoroughly, but the sketchbook was definitely not in the room.

Nancy drew Theresa aside while the others went downstairs. "Since last night, have you mentioned your suspicions about those shards to anyone?" she asked.

"No. I haven't said a word to anyone but you, Nancy." Theresa put a hand to her throat. "Maybe whoever was snooping around last night when we were talking took my sketchbook."

"My thoughts exactly," Nancy said quietly.

"But why?" Theresa wondered. "Who'd want my book?"

Nancy had no idea, but she was determined to find out.

An hour later in the woodworking barn, a dozen or so workshop participants were gathered around Andrea as she pointed out the specifics unique to colonial furniture.

Wood shavings littered the packed dirt floor, and the air was sweet with the smell of sawdust. Before the workshop Andrea had corralled some guys from around the village to help move the colonial chest from the curator's cottage to the wood shop. Now the simple chest stood on a skid in the middle of the floor, its surface gleaming softly with the patina particular to old wood.

Bess, with her passion for antiques, and George, with her love of woodworking, had signed up early to attend the demonstration and lecture on colonial furniture–making techniques. Nancy's motives were mixed. She liked Andrea and wanted to see her at work, but she also wanted to learn all she could about the way antiques had been made. Nancy was vaguely distressed by Andrea's obvious expertise and knowledge. Some of the smaller items bore a strong resemblance to some of the pieces Nancy had seen on buyersbeware.com. Of course, there were probably hundreds of woodworkers in the country who could pull off the fakes as well as, or better than Andrea. But hundreds of woodworkers were not in the neighborhood of those counterfeit pottery shards.

Nancy listened intently while Andrea explained some of the main ways to tell a genuine colonial piece of furniture from a good copy or a masterful fake. She was intrigued to learn that even knowledgeable dealers could be taken in.

"As you see here," Andrea ran her hand along the slightly ridged backboard, "the marks made by a wide-bladed jack saw can be easily felt. Try it, everyone."

Nancy joined the others, running her hand down

the broad wood plank. "How would a modern copy be different?" she inquired.

"Good question. Modern craftsmen use different tools. They smooth things down, trying to obscure tool marks." She stopped to point out sets of parallel scratches on the board. "Modern saws don't leave this kind of 'fingerprint.'" She picked up a board leaning against a nearby workbench. "I prepared this earlier, so you could compare the two. See how these saw marks form a wide arc? They come from a circular saw, which didn't exist in colonial times."

"So how come people are taken in by fakes?" a thin blond woman asked.

"Mainly because the people buying antiques aren't careful enough or don't know what to look for. Sometimes it's because they trust unscrupulous dealers."

"But if you wanted to fake something," Bess piped up, "wouldn't you use old tools, and mix up varnish just like the original? Like, you know everything there is to know about what goes into making a real colonial piece. You wouldn't make those sorts of mistakes."

Andrea colored slightly. "No, I wouldn't. But I don't have enough experience to pull off faking a dresser like this. Even if I did, I wouldn't. It's unethical."

"Still, Bess has a point," Nancy pushed the question. "Could you—or someone else with your know-how— make something good enough to fool an expert?"

Andrea hesitated, then with obvious reluctance nodded. "Up to a point. A few things couldn't be faked. Trees today aren't as big as the ones harvested for furniture in the 1700s. So the planks aren't as wide. Also, some of the materials in the varnishes just aren't available anymore. So chemical analysis would tip off whoever was looking at a piece carefully enough."

"But what about smaller pieces?" a gray-haired man asked. "Like candlesticks?"

Or lap desks, Nancy added silently, leaning forward to watch Andrea as she answered.

"Ah, well, that's easier, though you'd still have trouble with the patina and varnish," Andrea replied. "It would take a lot of talent to fool the big guns in the auction houses and museums."

Andrea continued her demonstration, leaving Nancy wondering about the woodworker. She liked Theresa's roommate and didn't want to suspect her of anything. Still, Andrea certainly knew the ropes well enough to make copies of smaller pieces. And Nancy suspected, in spite of Andrea's protests to the contrary, that she might be a good enough craftsperson to pull it off.

Nancy made a mental note to check out Andrea's résumé. Maybe she'd find some hint about how expert the young woodworker was.

After the workshop ended, the woodworking students lingered, talking to Andrea, while the girls headed out of the barn and into the late-afternoon sun. Nancy stopped at the head of the dirt path leading back toward Meadow House to check their schedule. The next raku workshop session, glaze making, wasn't until the next day, which would give her time to check out Andrea's résumé.

"Look at that. I wonder if he's getting chewed out for rescuing those quilts today," Bess said, pointing across the road.

Nancy followed the direction of Bess's gaze. Danny and Ellie May were huddled together. Danny was talking excitedly, pointing back up the road toward the farmhouse residence. He turned suddenly and saw Nancy. Flashing her a tight smile, he said something to Ellie May, then hurried off.

Nancy stared at his back. He was wearing a rather large backpack, like the kind used for camping trips.

George touched her arm and pointed to the backpack. "Do you see what I see?" she murmured.

"More than big enough for that sketchbook," Nancy remarked.

"Or for a lap desk," George suggested.

Overhearing that remark, Bess gasped softly. "And Danny had the perfect opportunity. Remember, he ran back into the house during the fire!"

9

Half Lies? Half Truth?

"Hi, girls. Enjoying the workshop?" Ellie May crossed the road toward Nancy and the girls.

"You bet," Bess enthused, smiling up at the tall woman. "It's just great, and this whole place is so incredible."

"The raku class is really cool," George added. "And I couldn't believe how much I learned just now, sitting in on Andrea's demonstration. I'm really glad we came."

Ellie May smiled benignly at Bess and George, then, shading her eyes, turned toward Nancy. "So, it turns out you and Theresa Kim are old friends. I didn't realize that."

The comment surprised Nancy. "I guess we are old friends, in a way. Our fathers are friends. We haven't seen each other in years." Nancy wondered why it mattered to the older potter.

"Do you know Theresa won a National Artisans Association grant for next year? She's the youngest winner ever. She leapfrogged over all the rest of us old-timers. Caused quite a stir in the ceramics community."

"She never even mentioned it," Nancy said, impressed. "But we've barely had time to talk."

"She's so busy," George interjected.

"That, too. But Theresa's rather close-mouthed about her career. You'll find she's just full of surprises," Ellie May concluded, then seemed to remember something. "In fact, have you read the article in *Today's Potter?* Theresa got quite an interesting write-up there. You should read it. It's in the library."

"I will," Nancy promised. "In fact, I might look at it now. I was heading in that direction anyway. After that demonstration I wanted to see what Andrea has on display in the store, and I thought I'd check her résumé."

"That's in the library, too. You can kill two birds with one stone, as they say."

Or maybe three, Nancy thought suddenly. What better place than the East River Junction library to find more detailed information about ceramic forgeries. Theresa didn't want Ellie May to know about the shards, but it couldn't hurt to feel out the older potter to get her input on the scam. "I was checking raku online the other night," Nancy started, "when I came across a web site called buyersbeware.com. I found out that lots of fake ceramic pieces have been hitting the collectibles market."

"Oh, *that!*" Ellie May gave a small grunt of disgust. "Isn't it awful? Everyone's talking about it, but who's doing anything about it?" she asked hotly, her drawl becoming more pronounced the more emotional she grew. "That's what I'd like to know." She cast an apologetic glance at Nancy. "Sorry, but that kind of cheating gets me positively hot under the collar. We're pretty honest, hardworking folks in general, Nancy."

"I know that, Ellie May," Nancy said. "And I hope whoever's behind this gets caught and gets exactly what's coming to them."

"Don't count on it," Ellie May warned grimly. "Forgers are not just good cheats; they're generally very clever at covering their tracks."

Nancy couldn't agree more. "So I guess it's off to the library to look up that article now."

"I'm heading in that direction myself," Ellie May said.

As Ellie May led the girls down a dirt path, Bess said, "You must have trouble keeping up with your own work. I haven't seen you at the pottery studio these two days."

Ellie May lifted her eyebrows. "I play catch-up with my own work after hours. I've been at my wheel long past your bedtime."

"I've noticed lots of people work late in the pottery studios," Nancy said casually. "Your assistants Michael and David were there late last night."

"Did they pull an all-nighter? I saw them this morning early when I went jogging," George contributed.

Ellie May shrugged. "Don't rightly know. I was in and out myself. Like the rest of us, they snatch any time they can to do their work." Turning toward Nancy again, Ellie May said, "Funny, I thought you'd be at the bonfire last night, not at the pottery studio. Did the clay bug bite you that hard?"

"No." Nancy managed a laugh, then quickly improvised. "I lost an earring during the workshop yesterday."

"Did you find it? In the dark?" Ellie May asked, looking at the gold studs in Nancy's ears.

"No. As you said, it was dark," Nancy answered. Did Ellie May know about her meeting with Theresa? Had one of her assistants seen Nancy around the studio?

"It wasn't against village rules or anything for Nancy to be there, was it?" Bess asked.

Ellie May laughed. "Of course not. It's just that it can be dangerous creeping around pottery yards at night in the dark. Anyway, girls, this is where I leave you. Enjoy the library, and don't forget that article about Theresa. I think it will be very enlightening!" With that, Ellie May jauntily walked away.

"What were you really doing at the pottery studio last night?" Bess prodded Nancy.

"Yeah, Nan, all we know is, you went to meet Theresa about some really hush-hush problem. Then you took off to River Heights this morning to go to the museum. I sense a mystery in the air," George said.

"And don't try to keep it from us," Bess warned playfully.

Nancy threw her hands up. "Okay, guys. I get it. You're feeling left out, but only because I haven't had a chance to let you in on what's happened." Then Nancy told them everything.

"Have you told Theresa what Mr. Darien said about the shards?" Bess asked as they walked into the curator's cottage.

As they stopped to sign the register of visitors in the hall outside the library, Nancy shook her head. "I had only one chance, but I forgot. I'll talk to her this evening. Meanwhile, maybe you guys can help."

"You want me to stake out the pottery studio after dark," George suggested eagerly.

"No." Nancy laughed softly as they walked into the

library. A couple of women Nancy recognized from Meadow House were at the card catalog.

"Why don't you and George look through some general craft magazines to see if you can turn up anything useful about counterfeiting, while I check out Andrea's résumé, and then look at *Today's Potter.*"

The girls split up, and Nancy quickly located the latest issue of *Today's Potter,* then picked up a loose-leaf binder with Junction residents' résumés.

Against the wall, next to the desk, Nancy saw a glass-front cabinet. A small sign inside the locked door read, Raku by Junction Staff. Nancy stopped to look at the display. Each shelf held the work of a different artist. The bottom shelf was full of sturdy-looking tea bowls. They were Danny's. Their casual, almost careless quality was appealing. Danny had even left the indentations where his thumbs had held the wet clay. But his raku pieces didn't even remotely resemble the thick-walled but refined forged raku piece Nancy had left with Mr. Darien.

Nancy proceeded to the alcove table where Bess and George were already seated, wondering if Danny had the touch to pull off the raku fakes. After seeing this small display of Danny's work, Nancy had her doubts.

After a few minutes of quiet reading, George whistled softly under her breath. "Hey, Nancy, look at this." She shoved a magazine across the mahogany table.

Nancy looked first at the spread that featured ornate silver tureens, as well as less showy pewterware. The headline read: "So You Want to Fake It?" When she saw the byline, her jaw dropped. "Jonathan wrote this?"

"Jonathan Walton himself," George confirmed. "I've already skimmed it. It points out all the mistakes counterfeiters make when they try to imitate colonial metalwork."

"Does *everyone* around here know all the tricks of the trade?" Bess remarked, peering over Nancy's shoulder at the article.

"It sort of makes sense," Nancy mused, turning the page and smiling slightly at the photo of Jonathan. He exuded the same combination of arrogance and cockiness that was at the same time appealing and off-putting.

George took back the magazine. "I guess he has a right to look smug. He seems to be a real expert in the field of identifying forgeries."

Nancy finished reading Andrea's résumé. She couldn't really tell much from it, except that Andrea had gone to Cranbrook, one of the most prestigious design schools in the country.

Next Nancy looked at *Today's Potter*. She found the article on Theresa under a monthly feature called "Up and Comings." The opening paragraph introduced Theresa as one of the leaders of a new generation of potters championing highly crafted, controlled, and refined work. "Tradition," the article went on, "is wedded seamlessly to a sense of the modern. This is no surprise, considering this ceramicist's background. Theresa Kim's expertise is not limited to the making of her wares; she can boast of a thorough education in and understanding of clay formulation and chemistry, as well as an internship during her college years, at the Boston Center for Far Eastern Studies in their restoration and conservation department."

Nancy reread that passage and shook her head in disbelief. No wonder Theresa did such a fine job putting together those shards. She had far more expertise than she had claimed. Why hadn't she mentioned her internship to Nancy? Nancy suddenly felt heartsick. Could it be Theresa was somehow involved in the scam? After all, raku pieces weren't the only ones being forged. Mr. Darien had reminded Nancy that all sorts of phony antique Korean and Chinese ceramics were hitting the market.

"Nancy!" Bess's cry cut in on Nancy's thoughts.

Nancy looked up. Bess had moved to the window seat nestled in the alcove. Next to her was a stack of oversize art books. She had a particularly thick one opened in front of her on the seat. "Nancy, didn't you say that all sorts of Asian ceramics are being forged?"

"Sure. Why?" Nancy asked as she and George got up to see what Bess was pointing at. Nancy looked at the title: *Far Eastern Ceramics*.

"Nancy, someone's torn the pictures out!" Bess exclaimed.

10

A Close Call

"Whoever cut out these pages wasn't very careful," Nancy observed. Though the edges of the missing pages were fairly straight, a good inch of paper stuck out from the binding. Nancy judged that at least eight pages had been cut, but she checked the page numbers to make sure. "They didn't bother to try to hide the damage," she surmised, "so they were probably in a rush."

"Do you think this is the book Danny was looking at the other day?" Bess asked with a frown.

"Could be," Nancy mused. "The book he dropped was large, about this size. But why would he bother tearing pages out of a book? He could have copied the pages just as easily."

"Right. I noticed a color photocopy machine by the checkout desk," George informed her.

Nancy sat down next to Bess on the window seat and thumbed through the thick art book at random. "Danny's stealing pages from a book just doesn't make sense to me. He—" She broke off suddenly and stared at a small black-and-white photo at the top of one page. It showed a simple shallow bowl. The shape was distinctive, modern, and eye-catching. Since the photo was black and white, Nancy couldn't tell the exact color of the bowl, though it was pale enough to be a creamy white. "Look at this!" she said.

"What's Theresa's pot doing in this book?" Bess wondered, touching the photo.

"It's not Theresa's," George said slowly. "The caption says it's a piece from eighteenth-century Korea."

Bess narrowed her eyes at Nancy. "Nancy Drew, tell me you're not thinking what I think you're thinking."

Very slowly and with great reluctance Nancy said, "I am. I think Theresa might be involved in the forgeries."

"Not on your life!" Bess cried, jumping up. The other people in the library looked up from their reading. Bess flashed a small, apologetic smile.

"It's possible," Nancy insisted, her voice low. Ticking off points on her fingers, she said softly, "Theresa has the expertise. She can easily make bowls that look like this expensive antique."

"Time out!" George interrupted, making a T with her hands. "It's time for a reality check, Nan. Theresa's the one who exposed the scam to you. She told *you* about the shards."

"Besides," Bess put in, "Theresa doesn't do raku, and as George said, she's the one who brought *you* the evidence."

Nancy leaned forward with her elbows on her knees and stared across the library. The other visitors had packed up their things and left. The library was quiet, and dust motes danced in the slanty beams of colored light pouring through the massive window. Nancy wanted to be wrong about Theresa, and maybe she was. But she had learned a long time ago to try not to let her personal feelings cloud her judgment. She liked Theresa, wanted her to be innocent, but wanting wouldn't make it so. "I hear you, Bess," Nancy said. "I hope you're right. But remember, her pot was in that raku barrel on Sunday, the one Danny found."

"I forgot about that," George said, curling her legs up under her on the seat. "Though she swore she had never put it in the barrel or raku fired it."

"Then who did? And why?" Nancy went on. "If Theresa's innocent, why didn't she tell me she was an expert in conservation and old materials?"

"She is?" Bess and George gasped in unison.

Nancy showed them the magazine article, then made them promise they wouldn't mention anything she'd found out that afternoon to Theresa. "And I'll put her off a bit longer about the museum and the curator. I keep forgetting how impressed he was with the way she had glued those shards together. He thought an expert had done the work."

"Okay, we'll keep our mouths shut," George promised. "But speaking of experts, maybe we should feel out some of the other teachers here. Isn't Jonathan giving a talk and demo tomorrow about his pewter work?"

"At two P.M.," Bess piped up.

"The girl has his whole schedule memorized," George marveled.

"That might conflict with the kiln-building session that everyone taking any pottery classes here is invited to join," Nancy said, frowning.

"I'll help with the kiln in the morning, but in the afternoon I'm going to check out Jonathan," Bess insisted.

"We'll *all* go. I want to draw him out a bit, since he knows so much about forgeries," Nancy said.

"What should we do about this book?" George asked, holding up the history of Asian ceramics.

"When and if I can find out who ripped out these pages and why, I'll speak to Ellie May," Nancy said.

Bess sounded hopeful, "So you think it might *not* be Danny?"

"I don't know," Nancy said, rubbing her head. "To tell you the truth, I'm so hungry and tired right now, I can't think straight. Let's go to dinner, and maybe things will be clearer on a full stomach."

The girls put away their magazines and went outside, where Bess checked her watch. "Hey, guys, I've got some really crummy news. We lost track of time in there. Unless we can beam back to the dining hall and go through some kind of time warp, we're twenty minutes past the end of the dinner period."

"I've got an idea, and it'll give us a chance to talk in private away from the village," Nancy said. "I'm sure I saw a pizza place in that mini-mall we passed between here and the interstate. Let's grab the car and head out that way."

A few minutes later the girls had piled into the Mustang and Nancy was driving down the narrow Junction road with the top down. Several small dirt roads branched off the blacktop. Nancy chose one of the dirts roads that Melinda had pointed out as a shortcut to town.

As Nancy stopped to turn off the two-lane blacktop, a vintage black pickup truck squealed around them, then peeled off down the dirt road, sending up a cloud of dust.

"Ugh!" Bess cried, fanning her face. "That was mean!"

"And dangerous," Nancy said. The truck was traveling much too fast down the rough road.

A few minutes later the three girls walked out of the warm evening into the cool air-conditioning of Pizza Heaven. A vintage 1950s jukebox was blaring a classic Chuck Berry tune. The place was packed. A large group of familiar faces could be seen at a back booth. George stopped in her tracks. "Is this party central or what?"

"Everyone from the Junction is here!" Bess exclaimed.

"Just the whole ceramics staff," Nancy corrected her. "I remember now. Theresa told us that on Thursday nights Ellie May takes her pottery crew, including the assistants and apprentices, out for pizza."

"Hey, look who's here!" Tom yelled, spotting Nancy. "Pull up a table and join us," he invited them.

Nancy hesitated, but Ellie May waved them over while Danny and Tom hauled a table up to one end of the booth to make more room. The girls pulled up chairs and settled in. Two steaming pies were already on one end of the table. Cans of soda and iced tea filled a big tray in the middle of the booth.

"Didn't think you'd get tired of Junction food so fast," Ellie May quipped, motioning toward the waiter. "Anything special on your pizza? My treat," she added. "We've got two more pies coming out now, but knowing this crew, we'll need another."

"Half pepperoni, half veggie," Bess requested slinging her bag on the back of her chair. "That way George doesn't have to eat the pepperoni, I can skip the veggies, and Nancy can have both!"

Nancy sat across from Danny and Ellie May and looked around. "Thanks for including us in your pizza party. I hear it's a regular Thursday night tradition."

"It's good for us staffers to get out, especially during the summer when things are busy."

The pizzas were served, and as Nancy ate she looked around and wondered why Theresa was missing. Theresa had hinted at feeling left out at the Junction, but would Ellie May exclude her on purpose? Then Nancy realized the two guys who were Ellie May's top assistants, the ones she'd seen in the studio the other night when she was talking with Theresa, had skipped the party, too.

"Too bad," Karen said, flipping her long dark braid over the back of her chair, "Michael and David couldn't come again tonight."

"They had to finish firing that kiln. You know it needs watching," Ellie May said. "Sorry the schedule's worked out that way for them. I'll take them their own personal pizza later."

"And Theresa? Is she firing a kiln, too?" Bess

asked, taking a slice of pizza and popping a piece of pepperoni in her mouth.

"Theresa?" Danny's laugh had an edge to it. "She's too good for the likes of us. She's not in charge of kilns, but she's always too busy to come."

"Or too bored or whatever," Karen spoke up from a corner of the booth.

"That's not fair, guys," Ellie May protested. "Theresa's just a bit of a workaholic. She reminds me of myself when I was young. She's just very driven, very determined."

"Determined to keep to herself," Tom remarked. "I can't tell if she's a snob, or shy."

"The girl is just very single-minded," Ellie May said. "How do you think she learned as much as she has about ceramics in such a short time? She's not even thirty, and she knows more than anyone in the village, including me, about glazes and firing techniques."

"Enough about Theresa." Danny abruptly shot a warning glance toward Ellie May. "I'm getting sick of hearing about how great she is."

"Jealous!" accused Tom.

"And *you* aren't?" Danny countered.

"Cool it, guys," Ellie May said, motioning toward the waiter. "Let's have another pie for here, and then one to go, with the works," she told him.

Nancy, Bess, and George stood and said they had

to leave. "What with the kiln building tomorrow, I'm going to need my rest," Nancy added.

Outside it was a little cool. Nancy slipped on her cardigan but left the car's top down. George climbed into the front passenger seat, and Bess stretched out in back.

Bess waited until they were out of the parking lot before asking, "Did you see the way Danny shut Ellie May up? What was that about?"

"It's pretty obvious that there's no love lost between Danny and Theresa—at least on Danny's side," Nancy said. But as she headed back toward the Junction, she entertained another, more disquieting thought. Ellie May had told Nancy that the whole ceramics community was talking about the forgeries. Probably everyone was eyeing everyone else with suspicion. If Danny *wasn't* one of the forgers, was it possible he suspected Theresa? On the other hand, if he somehow was able to pull off those forgeries, was he trying to frame her?

"Nancy, isn't this where we turn off?" George asked suddenly, pointing through the windshield.

Just ahead, in the beam of her headlights, Nancy saw the turnoff for a narrow dirt road.

"Thanks, George, I was sort of daydreaming," she admitted as she put on her directional signal, then turned. The road seemed narrower than on the way out and more deeply rutted. There were no shoulders to speak of, and the broad leaves of the tall field corn brushed the sides of the convertible.

"I don't remember the road being this bad!" Bess complained from the backseat.

"Me neither," Nancy agreed. "And I don't remember its forking like this," she added as the road split in two.

"Maybe you should turn around and go back to the highway," George suggested.

Nancy turned on her high beams. "I can't. There's not enough space. If we can spot the lights from the Junction, we'll just head in that direction. Melinda told me there's a virtual maze of dirt roads back here, but all of them converge down at the road that runs along the river and eventually connects up to the Junction blacktop."

"I think there's light down that way!" Bess pointed off to the right.

Nancy peered into the dark. Sure enough, a slight glow seemed to emanate from behind the tall corn. Nancy chose the right fork. The road was still rough but less rutted and a little wider. Soon the corn gave way to soybeans. Now Nancy could see clearly some distance ahead. There was no village. Instead Nancy found herself approaching a large barn. Floodlights tacked to the peak of the barn's tin roof illuminated the barnyard. A pickup truck with its lights on idled in front of the open barn doors. A radio droned a slow country ballad.

As Nancy approached she became aware that some guys were in the barnyard. They were hauling bales of hay from inside the barn, then putting them carefully into the back of the truck.

"Nan, isn't that the same truck we saw on our way to pizza?" George observed.

Nancy made a face. " 'Fraid so." She sighed.

"Maybe they're just rude drivers and not rude people." Bess sounded hopeful.

"Well, they can't be all that rude about giving simple directions," Nancy stated, then pulled into the barnyard. "At worst, we have a place to turn around."

Leaving the engine running, Nancy got out of the car and waved in the direction of the men. She jogged up toward them, a smile on her face.

"Hey there! We're lost." As she approached, the men froze in their tracks. Nancy saw there were four guys, though she couldn't make out their faces. One said something to his buddies. He started toward her while the others ducked back into the barn. Nancy went forward to meet him, shielding her eyes from the glare of the floodlights. "Does this road lead to East River Junction?" she asked. "Or should we turn around and head back to the highway?"

"What are you doing snooping around here, girlie?" the guy said gruffly, continuing toward her.

Nancy stopped but stood her ground. "I'm not snooping," she said firmly. "We're just lost."

"That's not my problem."

"Look, we're lost. If you'd just—" Nancy broke off as a chorus of growls sounded from the back of the truck. She began to back away, but before she could take more than a few steps, two snarling dogs leaped out of the pickup and charged toward her.

At the sight of the huge rottweilers Nancy froze.

"Nancy," George screamed from the car. "The dogs!"

Nancy sprang into action, turning back toward the car and breaking into a run.

"Put the top up!" she screamed at George as she pelted across the packed dirt of the barnyard. Nancy was a fast runner, but the dogs were faster. They were gaining on her. Several feet shy of the car, she could feel their breath on her back. "Let go!" she yelled as teeth sank into the loose fabric of her sweater.

11

A Dangerous Game

There was a terrible ripping sound as Nancy vaulted into the front seat of her car seconds before the convertible top closed down.

Nancy pounded the automatic window button. It whooshed closed as the dogs were flinging themselves at her door.

"Let's get out of here!" Bess shrieked from the backseat.

Pumped with adrenalin, Nancy threw the car into reverse. She gunned her engine, and the dogs backed off, growling. Then she swerved into a screechy U-turn and tore out of the barnyard.

Nancy's heart was racing as she glanced in her

rearview mirror. The narrow road stretched straight behind her, and the well-lit barnyard was still in sight. The dogs were holding their ground at the edge of the barnyard, barking furiously. Behind the dogs, silhouetted in the light, all four guys were standing near their pickup, staring at the Mustang.

"What if they follow us?" Bess shuddered in the backseat, where she was peering out the window.

"They don't seem to be in any rush," Nancy said, but she continued to speed down the bumpy road. Only when she reached the place where the road forked did she slow down and finally stop.

Nancy blew out her breath and rested her forehead on the steering wheel. "That was seriously scary," she said, lifting her head after a moment.

"They could have killed you, Nan," George said.

"Well, I'm okay." Nancy's pulse was finally slowing. She pulled off her sweater and eyed the hole ruefully. "Hannah made this for me," she said, putting it on the seat beside her and reaching for her seat belt. "Let's get out of here. I'm still not sure those creeps aren't going to follow us. This is a pretty dark, deserted road."

"But what was with those guys? You just asked for directions," Bess grumbled.

"Obviously, they didn't want to be disturbed. I have a feeling we walked in on something illegal. Otherwise why the dogs? Why the attitude?" Nancy said.

Driving more carefully to avoid the ruts, Nancy replayed the scene in her head. Something about those guys and that truck was bothering her. Suddenly she knew what. She glanced across the front seat at George. "Did you notice anything weird about the way those guys were loading hay in that truck?"

"Like what?"

"Like, they were handling those hay bales like they were made of glass. Usually you just throw bales into the back of a truck or a wagon. You don't carry them as if they're fragile cargo."

"Nancy, come to think of it, you're right. It was weird."

"But why would they do that?" Bess wondered.

"I'm not sure," Nancy said, although she had a pretty good hunch. Still, she wanted to keep it to herself until she was more certain. "But I tell you one thing, I'm going back there tomorrow night to check it out."

"Are you nuts?" George gasped. "What about those dogs?"

"I'll figure something out. Maybe I'll drop by that BurlyBurgers joint in town and pick up some burgers to go. Or I'll go to the supermarket and buy a couple of steaks to keep them busy. But don't worry. I'll be careful."

The next morning Nancy arrived early at the pottery studio. The air was heavy and still. Though it was barely eight, the sky was hazy. The day promised to be hot and humid. Outside the studio, someone had improvised a table from an old door and two sawhorses. A cheerful plastic cloth was draped across the top. The studio coffee urn had been moved outside, and now it bubbled next to a tray heaped with bagels. Nancy took a cup of coffee.

The pottery yard had been cleaned up since the other night. Raku barrels were stacked in an open storage shed. Woodpiles had been straightened out. The clutter of buckets and hoses and other raku paraphernalia had been stowed away. Looking pasty and half asleep, Karen yawned a "good morning" to Nancy, then went back to sorting a skid of bricks.

The kiln-building workshop wouldn't begin for half an hour or so. Ellie May's drawl floated out from the studio as she issued orders to her helpers. Nancy caught only a few words, something about firebricks, lathing, and work gloves. Nancy started for the studio door, in half a mind to report the incident at the barn to Ellie May. Nancy was angry, annoyed, and still a bit shaken. But she was also wary. Those men had been up to no good. Why were they loading bales of hay onto a truck after ten at night anyway?

Nancy backed away from the studio and poured herself more coffee. She'd put off talking to Ellie May. The acting director might be forced to call in the police if Nancy lodged a formal complaint about the dogs. Nancy wanted the chance to investigate that barn herself first. Something had to be inside those bales of hay—some kind of contraband. Why else would the guys be so defensive? All she had done was ask for directions.

No, whatever was stashed in those hay bales had to be illegal. Maybe the guys were fencing stolen goods or even drugs. But Nancy would bet anything that they were moving counterfeit pots—pots that had been made here in the village, perhaps by Danny but most likely by Theresa, she concluded sadly. "I hope I'm wrong," she murmured aloud.

"About what?" Ellie May asked, approaching the coffee urn.

Nancy felt her cheeks grow red. "Sorry. I don't usually mutter to myself," she said with an embarrassed laugh. Then to change the subject, she said, "I checked out the raku display in the library yesterday. I liked your pieces."

"Why, thank you." Ellie May looked pleased.

"Do you do lots of raku?" Nancy asked.

"Sometimes." Ellie May's tone became guarded. "Especially here. Why?"

"I'm just curious," Nancy admitted. "All you potters—like the ones with works on display in that library case—have distinctive styles. I'd never mistake your work for Theresa's or Danny's."

Ellie May studied Nancy before answering. "It's partially out of choice, depending on which process you enjoy doing most. A well-trained ceramic artist can do fairly controlled work, as well as looser pieces, though I think a person's innate talent steers them in one direction or another. Does that answer your curosity?"

Nancy laughed. "Perfectly," she said, but she watched Ellie May as the potter began to round up the students milling about the yard. Why had her questions put Ellie May a bit on the defensive?

"Sorry we're so late," George said, walking up to the table and snagging a bagel. "But Bess had trouble putting together a perfect kiln-building outfit."

Nancy looked at Bess and grinned. While George and she were dressed in jeans and fairly shabby T-shirts, Bess was wearing tan shorts and a cropped red stretch top that showed her navel. Her one concession to kiln building seemed to be her shoes: instead of platform sandals, Bess was wearing a pair of sparkly red high-top sneakers.

"I thought Theresa would be here," George commented, selecting a pair of work gloves from a stash on the table. She tossed a pair to Nancy.

Tucking them into her back pocket, Nancy said, "I ran into her this morning on my way over here. She was jogging back from the river to the residence. She said she was still trying to reconstruct her lost pottery notes. She's pretty upset about her sketchbook. Maybe she'll drop by later."

Bess looked up from trying to match a pair of gloves to her red top and dropped her voice. "Did you talk to her yet about what the museum curator said? She must be dying to know what you found out."

"No, I'd rather wait."

Before Nancy could say more, Ellie May called the group together. Nancy saw that Ellie's assistants, Michael and David, had turned up to help.

Both guys looked seriously rumpled as they reported to Ellie May. Nancy watched as they spoke with her. Michael suddenly caught Nancy staring at him. She smiled, but he turned away quickly. What's with him? Nancy wondered. She'd barely said two words to the guy since arriving at the Junction.

Ellie May talked about the different types of kilns. There were electric kilns, like the ones inside the studio. Others, fueled by gas, ranged from the small raku kiln to the large walk-in gas kiln housed in a separate outbuilding behind the main studio. "Then we have wood-burning kilns, like the kind you are building today. Here at the Junction we generally build a wood kiln during the summer workshops, then dismantle it at the end of the season and reuse the materials the next year for the next group of students. We also have the mother of all wood-burning kilns here, which I'm sure you saw on your tour of the village. It's called an anagama kiln. Ours has six chambers climbing into the side of a hill. It's very large, and is fired only two or three times a year. It's a permanent structure. If you get a chance over the next couple of days, check it out."

Ellie May went on to explain the process of building a simple kiln. "First we lay down a base or foundation of cinder blocks. Let me warn you now, you women are to lift the blocks in pairs . . ."

George groaned in protest. "Hey, some of us are strong."

"Right. I'm sure you are strong enough, but it's crucial to save your back."

George rolled her eyes as Ellie May continued, "On top of the blocks we'll lay down several courses, or rows, of hard bricks, then we'll switch to the softer firebricks. The tough part is the arch, but fortunately this is a small kiln. You see we already have the arch form built of wood over there. Hard brick is used for the arch.

"It'll all be clearer once you look at our plan and some photos of a completed kiln—the one we built last year." Ellie May gathered everyone around a table to look at the plan and the pictures. She finally concluded. "It's pretty small-scale, and with a crew of—let's see, you're about a dozen—we should finish the work this afternoon, or by early evening at the latest. I know some of you are just more or less visiting this workshop, so you're free to leave whenever you want." Next she divided people into teams, assigning one studio helper to each pair of students. Nancy found herself teamed with Ellie May.

Soon the work began, and time seemed to fly. Heaving the cinder blocks, even in teams, proved to be tiring, but by the time the fourth course of hard bricks was laid, Nancy, sweaty and with her face streaked with dust, realized she was having a great time. She swigged down some water and ran her arm across her forehead. Looking around, she saw that all the participants were smiling, dirty, and thoroughly enjoying themselves.

"Speaking of firebricks, we need some more," Ellie May said. She started across the yard toward a row of skids stacked tall with pale-colored bricks. "Nancy, I could use a hand."

Nancy put down her water and hurried over to help.

Ellie May flashed a grateful smile as Nancy piled a stack of lightweight bricks into the woman's arms. Ellie May headed toward the kiln while Nancy stayed behind a moment to pick up some bricks that had fallen on the ground.

Suddenly Nancy heard a strange grating noise. She glanced up just as George shouted, "Nan, watch out!" At the same time the tall pile of bricks slipped off the skids and tumbled toward her.

12

Whispers and Rumors

The brick pile teetered on the skids, then collapsed toward Nancy. She dove to the side, hitting the ground hard facedown and throwing her arms over her head. The bricks landed with a crash, sending up a cloud of dust, just to the right of where Nancy lay.

"Nancy!" George cried, racing to her side. "Are you all right?"

"Don't move," Ellie May cried, running to join them. "Did you break anything?"

"I-I'm fine," Nancy managed. She ran a hand down her forearm and winced.

"You're bleeding!" Bess exclaimed.

"I just got scraped," Nancy said, getting up. "I'm

fine, Ellie May. Nothing some soap and water and a bandage won't fix."

Ellie May shook her head vehemently. "That's a pretty nasty scrape. I'll have someone take you down to the curator's cottage. You could use some antibiotic ointment on that once you clean it up."

"I'll go with Nancy," Bess volunteered.

"You could have been killed if those bricks had beamed you!" Danny remarked.

"It was just an accident," Nancy said, feeling a little sore.

As Bess went to get Nancy's small backpack from the studio, George commented, "An accident? I guess so, but one that could have been prevented. Someone was behind those bricks just before they fell."

"I'm almost sure I also saw someone walk back there a minute before the bricks fell," Danny admitted. He checked out the remaining piles. "Not that anyone would knock them over on purpose, of course."

George exchanged a quick glance with Nancy. "Of course not," she said.

While Danny and the crew cleaned up the mess, Nancy motioned for George to follow her. As soon as they were out of earshot, she said softly, "I'm sure this was no accident. Not after last night. I bet whoever's behind this knew about our discovering that truck at the barn."

"But who? Danny's one of your prime forgery suspects, but he wasn't anywhere near those skids. He was standing next to me when they fell, Nancy."

Nancy studied the layout of the skids. They were lined up in front of two of the woodsheds. There was certainly space between the sheds and the skids for someone to hide. And making a quick getaway was easy in the maze of small buildings. She was tempted to search the whole area, but she didn't want to draw more attention to herself. "Do you know if it was a guy or a girl?"

George pursed her lips. "I think it was a guy, though I can't swear to it."

Nancy stooped to check the ground behind the skids, but the dirt was packed hard and too dry for any footprints to be visible. Whoever had been lurking behind the skids hadn't left a trace. As Nancy stood up, her eye caught the gleam of something metallic half hidden beneath the skid. Quickly she dropped down and pulled out a metal ring. It looked like a circular key ring but was larger than most. Instead of keys, it held an assortment of different-size brass rings.

"What's that?" George asked.

"Nancy, have you gone for first aid yet?" Ellie May called out.

"I'm leaving now, with Bess," Nancy replied, quickly pocketing the large ring. To George she added, "I have no idea what this is. Maybe it's a clue. Maybe whoever was hanging out back here dropped it. Or maybe it's been there for days. I'll have to find out."

Nancy joined Bess and started for the curator's cottage. George walked them a few feet down the road. "You still going to the pewter workshop at one?" she asked.

"Yes. I want to feel out Jonathan. He knows a lot about antiques and forgeries. Maybe we can learn something from him," Nancy explained.

"I'll pass, if you don't mind," George said. "I want to see the kiln finished. Meanwhile I can keep an eye out for anything suspicious."

Nancy cast George a grateful look. "That's a *very* good idea!"

By afternoon the heat was stifling, and tall thunderclouds were building over the western horizon. After bandaging Nancy's arm, the girls had cleaned up a bit, grabbed lunch in the dining room, and headed over to the metal shop. It was housed in a low modern building, and when Bess opened the door she was greeted by a blast of cold air.

"Air-conditioning!" Bess was overjoyed. "I thought the Junction didn't believe in it."

"But our students do," Jonathan quipped as the girls walked into the studio. He wore a Cubs baseball cap, bill turned backward, and had a leather apron over his work shirt and jeans. "This new shop was well funded." Jonathan noticed Nancy's arm. "You look like a wall walked into you or something."

"Funny you should say that," she replied as he guided them over to a long worktable. "There was an accident over at the pottery studio this morning. I seem to have survived a close encounter of the fire-brick kind."

"But you seem to be okay." He ushered them toward two stools. "You're a lot tougher than you look."

Nancy arched her eyebrows. "I'll take that as a compliment."

Jonathan responded with a rakish smile.

Nancy took a seat and looked around. The studio was very large. At one end jewelry students were working at high tables. Most wore some kind of magnifying glass, which Nancy knew was called a loupe, over one eye.

This end of the studio boasted a bank of tall locked glass cabinets. Arranged inside were gleaming silver tea and coffee services, candelabras, and footed bowls. Some designs were clearly modern. Nancy thought others looked ornate and fussy in an old-fashioned way.

A glowing array of copper teakettles, pewter jugs and tankards, candlesticks, and trays were displayed at one end of the table.

"Are some of these old?" Bess asked, picking up a

copper teakettle and reverently running her finger down the lustrous spout.

"Not a one," Jonathan said. "We have some real valuable antiques up in the curator's cottage. These were all made here by me or other craftspeople." He offered them each a handout. Nancy saw it was a photocopy of his article on spotting fakes that she had seen in the library. "This might give you some idea of how pre-nineteenth-century metalsmiths fashioned their work. I'll wait a few minutes longer for the stragglers before beginning."

"Let's look around," Nancy suggested, easing herself off the high stool.

After glancing at the display of silver items, Nancy turned her attention to a peg board full of tools. She was testing the weight of a mallet when Bess let out a startled cry. "Nancy! Look at this!" Bess reached up and took a large metal ring off a hook. Dangling from it were smaller brass rings of various sizes. "It's just like the ring you found near those skids this morning."

"Did I hear something about a ring?"

Both girls turned. Jonathan had materialized behind them. "I lost one just like this last night, over by the pottery studio. I had it in my pocket when some of the guys asked me to help clean up the pottery yard and stack those firebricks."

Nancy struggled to keep her expression neutral. The ring belonged to Jonathan. Somehow he had to be involved in the counterfeit scheme. How deeply, Nancy wasn't sure, but she suspected that he was involved enough to try to hurt her.

Nancy reluctantly reached into her back pocket. "I had no idea what it was." She smiled at him sweetly, but her mind was racing. George had said it was a guy that she glimpsed behind the pile of bricks. The only male suspect Nancy had at the moment was Danny, who had been in plain sight when the "accident" occurred. Now Jonathan was claiming he owned the only clue Nancy had.

Would he be so open about it if he had really tried to harm Nancy? Or could he possibly be telling the truth? Had he actually lost the big ring the night before? Nancy decided she'd go back to the pottery studio after the workshop and quiz Ellie May about who had been working late.

Jonathan took the ring from Nancy and hung it back up on the peg board. "Thank you for saving me a lot of work and trouble. Those rings are used for sizing jewelry, among other things." Jonathan invited the girls back to the table, where he began his lecture.

A couple of hours later Bess and Nancy left the metal shop. The sky had darkened, and thunder rumbled in the distance. "I thought I would die in there when Jonathan said those rings were his," Bess confided as she and Nancy started across the field toward Meadow House. "Nan, is Jonathan mixed up in all of this?"

"I'm not sure," Nancy admitted. "But I'm going to check something out now. Why don't you go find George and see if she heard or saw anything suspicious. I'll catch up with you guys later, after dinner. I'm going to explore that barn in a while."

Thunder continued to rumble as Nancy silently prayed, Let the rain hold off. She had to wait until dark before she started snooping, so meanwhile a couple of questions to Ellie May would settle whether Jonathan was telling the truth.

As Nancy approached the studio from the back, she heard voices from inside. Staying out of sight, she peeked in the half-open window. Andrea was facing Danny.

"Danny, all I want is a simple yes or no for an answer. Has anyone *ever* approached you to fake antique raku pots?"

Nancy's pulse quickened. Just as she suspected, someone was luring Junction personnel into the lucrative forgery trade.

Danny's tone was defensive. "No way. Why won't you listen to me? No one's even bothered. *I'm* not famous enough. Anyway, what's it to you?"

After a moment's hesitation Andrea answered in a soft, worried voice, "I *have* been approached—several times already this summer."

Danny's face registered pure shock. "By whom? How?"

Andrea shrugged. "I have no idea. I was contacted by e-mail."

"So what did you do?"

Andrea straightened up. "What kind of person do you think I am, Danny Acero? I told them, no way. And I'm not the only person around here who's been approached."

"Who else?" Danny asked sharply.

Andrea bit her lip and shook her head sadly. "She doesn't know I know, but Theresa was, too."

13

All That Glitters

"So it's true!" Nancy blurted out, wishing with all her heart she had been wrong about Theresa. But the pieces of the puzzle fell all too neatly into place. "But why?" Nancy punched her fist against the building wall. Theresa had so much to lose if she were caught.

"Danny, someone's out there!" Andrea exclaimed from inside the pottery studio.

"I didn't hear anything," Danny grumbled, "but I'll check."

Pressing herself against the wall of the building, Nancy crept back toward a pool of deep shade cast by the trees. She heard the sound of a window being raised and froze, trying to meld with the shadows.

She saw a head poke out. The person looked toward the right, then turned in Nancy's direction but peered out toward the woodshed and not back along the side of the building. "I don't see anyone." Danny's voice carried out to Nancy.

He ducked his head back in. "You're so paranoid now you're hearing things" were the last words Nancy could make out.

Heartsick, Nancy went the long way around to the lot where her car was parked. For once she was wishing she could have been wrong about a suspect. Still, her experience solving mysteries had taught her not to let her personal feelings interfere with finding the truth. But as she climbed into her Mustang, she felt confused, angry, and hurt that Theresa had used her.

Forty-five minutes later, after the sun had set, the storm was about to break. Nancy retraced the route she'd accidentally taken the night before. The surface of the road seemed even more deeply rutted than she remembered.

As Nancy pulled into the barnyard, the storm broke. She hesitated, then pulled the car up closer to the barn, where it wouldn't be as visible from the road, and turned off the ignition. Then, grabbing her bag and a paper sack of burgers for the dogs, she threw open her door and made a dash for the back of the barn.

She ducked under the eaves, her T-shirt soaked and clinging to her. Nancy realized all at once that the dogs weren't there. To be on the safe side, she whistled softly. No dogs turned up.

A good omen, she thought, staying under the shelter of the eaves and moving around the barn. At the back she stopped abruptly. Half of the double barn door was closed, but the far half was open and swinging wildly in the wind. Cautiously Nancy tiptoed toward the open door and peeked inside.

A small, battery-powered lantern was propped up on a bale of hay. And kneeling in front of another bale, her back toward Nancy, was Theresa Kim.

"What are you doing?" Nancy cried, dismayed.

Theresa turned around, pure terror on her face. "Nancy!" she exclaimed, relief washing over her delicate features. "Am I glad to see you!"

Nancy stared at her. Theresa made no effort to conceal the tall porcelain pot cradled in her hands.

For a moment Nancy was speechless. "I wouldn't be glad to see me right now, if I were you!" Nancy countered coolly.

Theresa's smile dimmed. She shook back her hair and carefully put down the pot. "Why?"

Nancy couldn't believe the girl was still playing dumb. "Because I've caught you in the act, for one thing."

Theresa's expression slowly shifted from confused

to amazed. "You think *I* have something to do with this? I swear, you've got it all wrong."

"Do I?" Nancy moved slightly to block the entrance. She had no idea what Theresa would do, but she wanted to keep her here until she heard the whole story. "How about the part where you didn't let on that you knew all about antique Asian pots and were an expert at conservation? You very conveniently forgot to mention that you are an expert in formulating clay bodies—oh, and by the way, Theresa, Mr. Darien at the museum said the clay in the shards you supposedly found had been very cleverly formulated to resemble the clay used in old pots."

Theresa closed her eyes and pressed her hands against her face.

"You forged pots, Theresa, and tried to pull me into your game—to use me as cover."

Theresa had dropped her hands and was staring at Nancy aghast. "Use you as cover? Nancy, I didn't. And I have never forged a pot in my life—*never!*" she declared, angrily wiping away tears. "I can't believe you actually suspect me."

Theresa looked so righteous and offended that Nancy suddenly felt a prick of doubt. Was there more to this story? But what? And then she remembered what she'd just overheard. "You also forgot to mention being approached on your e-mail by whoever's behind this scam."

"How do you know about that?" Theresa sank down heavily on a bale of hay.

"Andrea told Danny all about it," Nancy said, a pang of pity softening her tone.

"She has been hanging around a lot lately when I'm doing e-mail. That's why I cut off so suddenly that night when we were online together, Nancy. I didn't want her to see what I was writing. And yes, I have the skill to create forgeries—I admit it. Everyone knows I do. But after I turned down the offer in no uncertain terms, I began getting weird threats about my career hitting the skids. Then when that raku pot turned up in Danny's barrel last Sunday, that was the last straw. I figured it was put in the barrel to make people suspect that I was one of the artists involved." Theresa heaved a huge sigh and shook her head sadly. "Not that you'll ever believe me. And if you won't, no one will."

Nancy tried to digest Theresa's story. For a moment the only sound in the barn was the hum of the lantern, and the roar of the storm outside. "I suppose you're going to tell me that someone stole your sketchbook to get back at you for turning down the work."

"Worse than that. I think they want to blackmail me with it." Theresa continued with evident reluctance, "The book was full of sketches of examples of old pots that I was studying either from books or in museums. Stuff like this," she said, and reached over for the pot she had been holding earlier. "This is a very masterful fake—and if you look in my sketchbook you'll find a drawing exactly like it."

Nancy nodded slowly. "This does make sense."

"So you believe me?" Theresa asked, a note of hope in her voice.

"I'm trying to," Nancy admitted wryly. "But if you aren't involved in the scheme, how come you're here tonight? How did you know you'd find pots in these hay bales?"

"I followed two of the studio assistants here last night."

"Michael and David," Nancy guessed.

"You knew?"

"I just figured it out," Nancy admitted. "What made you suspect them?"

Theresa leaned forward and confided, "A couple of weeks ago I noticed they were the only two assistants who *never* went to Ellie May's pizza nights. Anyway, I followed them last night. They took the river road over here, then met up with two men in a pickup truck. I wanted to hang around, but those guys had some really scary dogs. So I cleared out. This barn isn't far from where I found those shards. If someone was moving pots out of here illegally, maybe he broke some and needed to hide any potential evidence. So I was pretty sure I'd find stuff like this here if I looked hard enough.

"Anyway, some of the stuff I found here tonight," she said, reaching over to a group of pots lying on their sides in the hay, "has been fired in the anagama kiln. There aren't many of those around, and even the one at the village is fired only two or three times a year. It's being fired starting Sunday night, when the anagama workshop starts. Someone could easily put their pieces in it without anyone noticing."

Nancy sighed. "I owe you an apology, Theresa." Nancy meant what she said, but part of her was still a bit wary. If Theresa wasn't the culprit, who was? Danny? "So what do you think is going on here, Theresa?"

Theresa's answer was guarded. "I don't want to accuse anyone, but I think a Junction potter is involved."

"A Junction potter?" Nancy repeated. "Like Danny?"

"Danny?" Theresa's head snapped up. "Danny couldn't make these pots. Not in a hundred years."

"He's not good enough?" Nancy asked.

"Well, if you put it that way—no, he's not. And he knows it."

Nancy blew out her breath. Picturing Danny's pots, she was pretty sure Theresa was right. Then she got an idea. Looking around the stall, she saw that Theresa had cut open only two or three bales. "Did you find anything else, Theresa, besides these pots?"

"No, why?"

"Come on, grab your lantern." Nancy headed out of the stall. She flicked on her own flashlight and shone it into the corners of the barn. The floor was strewn with loose hay, but in one corner hay bales were stacked very neatly, only two bales high. "There!" Nancy declared. She hurried over to the corner and knelt on the hard dirt floor. With her pen knife she loosened the straps holding the hay together.

"What are you looking for, Nancy?"

Instead of answering, Nancy dug her hand deeper into the bale and pulled out a pewter pitcher. "This!" she said, flourishing it under Theresa's nose. "Look in those bales there and see what you find."

After ten minutes Nancy sat back on her heels and surveyed the collection in front of her: more pots, raku and porcelain and wood-fired jugs; pewter and copper candlesticks; and finally a wooden lap desk. Theresa held her lantern above the little desk. "How did this get here?"

"Andrea was also approached by the counterfeiters," Nancy informed her. "My bet is that a lot of people at the Junction have been. Jonathan must have been—and believe me, I'm sure he's involved in this scam. He must have known I stumbled on this barn and the truck last night." Nancy told Theresa about the "accident" at the kiln that morning.

"Jonathan?" Theresa nodded. "Now, he's good enough to pull off anything. I don't know enough about metalwork to tell if this is a fake, but he knows enough to conjure up the old materials. I do know that lead solder isn't used anymore, but I'm sure he could get hold of lead and make solder good enough to fool most folks."

While Theresa talked, Nancy held Andrea's lap desk up to the light. She ran her fingers down the unfinished board at the back of the little desk. She could feel ridges, the kinds of marks Andrea had talked about earlier. "I don't think this is fake," Nancy said.

"It's not!" Theresa insisted. "Andrea is very proud of it. It's worth so much money she's crazy to carry it around with her, but she sees it as some kind of good-luck charm."

"Is it worth more than a good fake?"

"You bet it is," Theresa said. "And Andrea would no more fake a piece than I would, Nancy. Even though she might be good enough. But I tell you what. I think someone might think it's a fake and be trying to frame Andrea—"

A loud bang cut her off in midsentence.

Both girls jumped. "Just the barn door banging shut in the wind," Nancy said, hurrying over to check it. She pushed against it, but it didn't give.

Nancy yelled over to Theresa, "Come on over. I think it's jammed."

Theresa ran up to the door. She threw her shoulder against it, while Nancy pushed with both hands. The door didn't budge.

"What's going on?" Theresa looked wild-eyed at Nancy.

"Someone has locked us in!"

14

Tinderbox

Lightning flashed, the white light visible through chinks in the barn wall. Thunder boomed and the building shook slightly. "Locked in?" Theresa gasped.

Nancy aimed her flashlight at the crevice where the two doors met. "Someone must have bolted it from the outside," she said. "We're stuck."

"Who locked us in?" Theresa asked, pressing her back to the door and searching Nancy's face.

"I don't know for sure. I only hope it's not the guys I ran into last night." Another terrible thought occurred to her. Maybe Jonathan had followed her here somehow. He'd already tried to hurt her today. Well, she wasn't going to give him a second chance.

Frantically she swept the beam of her flashlight around the barn. "There must be another door or a window somewhere up in the loft. We've got to get out of here, Theresa, before whoever did this comes back."

Theresa held up her lantern while Nancy searched for a way up to the loft. Finally she spied a ladder. It took all of Nancy's strength to drag it over to the loft.

"Nancy, it barely reaches high enough," Theresa warned as Nancy mounted the first rung.

"Barely, but it does reach. Here, hold my flashlight while I climb." Nancy scaled the ladder slowly, the rungs creaking dangerously with every step. At the top she scrambled onto the loft floor. The rain drummed against the tin roof, but the loft was dry. "The light, Theresa," she called down hoarsely.

Theresa threw the light up to the loft. "There's a big door up here," Nancy yelled down to Theresa. "We can get out this way." The door was latched on the inside. Nancy threw the bolt, and the door swung out over the barnyard. It was a sheer drop—too high to jump.

Disheartened, Nancy tried to pull the heavy door shut, but it had swung out too far. "Forget it," she grumbled, then yelled down to Theresa. "No luck. It's too high."

Theresa's face fell, then brightened. "But what if

we could find some rope? You could climb down and unbolt the door from the outside."

"Good thinking," Nancy congratulated her. "I'll check up here again."

The wind banged the open door against the side of the barn, and sheets of rain swept in. A sudden flash of light caught Nancy's eye. It was steady, unlike lightning. A car, she realized. Nancy's blood ran cold. What if it was whoever locked them in the barn? She edged toward the open door and looked down.

Three figures in slickers were climbing out of a Jeep. Then over the howl of the wind Nancy heard a wonderfully familiar voice ring out over the barnyard.

"Nancy, are you in there?" Bess shouted.

"Yes," Nancy yelled down, leaning out of the window. "We're locked in. Unbolt the door, hurry!"

A moment later Nancy was back on the barn floor, hugging Bess and George. "You two are a sight for sore eyes!" Nancy said, relief making her feel weak in the knees. She drew back from the hug and found herself staring at Andrea. "Andrea, what are you doing here?"

"I know, Nancy, we weren't supposed to tell anyone, but Andrea's no forger, and we were worried about you," Bess babbled. "So I asked her to drive us here."

Andrea was shaking her head sadly. "I knew it" was all she said. She turned to Nancy and handed her a baseball cap. It had a Chicago Cubs logo. "I found this outside, under the eaves."

Nancy took the cap and noted it was barely wet. "Can't have lain there long. Whoever locked us in probably dropped it."

"That's Danny's," Theresa gasped.

"Or Jonathan's," Nancy answered.

"Jonathan?" Andrea looked skeptical. "Why would he lock you in a barn?"

"Because of this," Nancy said, leading Andrea and the other girls to the pewter pitcher.

Andrea sank down on a bale of hay. "Well, if this is a fake, he is the only person around here who could pull off something like this."

"And I think that explains the mystery of your desk," Theresa spoke up. "We found that here, too." Andrea jumped up and grabbed it. "How did this get here?"

"I'm not sure," Nancy said. "Jonathan could have been lurking inside the house during the fire, waiting to steal it. And it had to be either Danny or Jonathan who locked us in here. They both wear Cubs hats."

"Well, it wasn't Danny," Andrea declared. "He did take Theresa's sketchbook. Don't look so shocked, Theresa. He was sure you were involved in something shady from the get-go. He showed it to me and Ellie May earlier this evening. Ellie May took the sketchbook as evidence. If I know her, the police are probably on their way to the Junction now."

Theresa paled. "Andrea, it's not me. I didn't forge

anything, ever. I explained to Nancy about those drawings."

"Sure, and I bet your good friend here actually fell for your lies."

"Stop it, Andrea," Nancy said, intervening. "You have it all wrong. I'm pretty sure I know who's behind all this."

"Forget it, Nancy," Theresa cried hotly. "I told you no one would believe I was innocent. I'll just have to prove it myself." With that Theresa burst into tears and ran out of the barn.

"Come back here!" Nancy and Andrea both yelled. Nancy raced out of the barn into the storm. The lightning and thunder were moving off to the east, but the rain continued to fall in sheets. "Theresa!" Nancy yelled into the storm. She couldn't see a thing.

After a minute Nancy ducked back into the barn.

She turned to Andrea. "You're wrong about Theresa. I'm sure of that now. I'm heading back to the village to see if I can find her. Whoever locked us in this barn knows she's onto them. Her life might be in danger."

Then she pulled George aside. "George, keep Andrea away from Ellie May."

"But what about the police?" George asked.

Nancy let out a tight laugh. "Oh, I don't think they'll be turning up anytime soon."

*　*　*

125

The studio radio was tuned to a late-night jazz station. Some women were throwing pots on wheels toward the back of the room. Nancy ambled in and walked up and down the aisles of shelves. One of the women spotted Nancy and lifted a clay-covered hand in greeting. Nancy waved back. "Nice pot!" she said, admiring the tall cylinder. "Oh, by the way, have you seen Theresa?" The woman shook her head. Nancy crossed the floor and saw that there were people in the glaze room. She poked her head in.

Michael looked up. Beneath a dusty apron he was wearing cutoffs and a T-shirt with the sleeves rolled up. "Oh," he said. Was it her imagination, or did he sound surprised?

Just then David sauntered in, a large, beautiful jug in his hand. It was buff colored, only bisque fired and unglazed, but Nancy could see it was a twin to one of the anagama fired pots Theresa had just discovered back at the barn. "Wow," she said, moving closer. "That's really beautiful. Is that yours?" Nancy looked up at David from under her eyelashes.

"Don't I wish!" David rolled his eyes but looked flattered. "I'm just glazing it. This is by a real pro and—"

"David," Michael called out. "No time to gab, D. We've got to load that kiln tomorrow." Michael flashed Nancy a fake smile.

She smiled back broadly. "Oh, sorry. Didn't mean

126

to bother you," she murmured. Then with a little wave she ambled out of the glaze room.

Next stop, Nancy told herself, the anagama kiln. It was only a short walk down the road from the main studio. Nancy stopped at her car and grabbed her flashlight. She walked down the gravel drive leading back toward the road.

Suddenly Nancy got a prickly sensation at the back of her neck. She slowed down, then stopped. Behind her she heard the distinctive crunch of gravel. She flicked on her flashlight and spun around. Animal eyes glittered behind her. "A raccoon!" She laughed out loud, then continued on her way.

Nancy reached the anagama kiln a few minutes later to the din of peepers and the croak of frogs. Fireflies flickered everywhere, and a barrage of moths and other insects frantically mobbed a single outdoor light tacked to one wall of a three-sided shed. Nancy flicked off her flashlight and looked around. Several cords of wood were stacked near the kiln. The woodpile was covered with a blue plastic tarp, weighted down with large, heavy stones. Puddles of rainwater glistened on top of the tarp.

The kiln loomed large in the dark. Nancy remembered Melinda's explaining that it had four arch-roofed chambers. Where pots were placed in the kiln determined how they would look after firing was finished. Nancy hadn't paid much attention to the technical details, but she did remember that the kiln held lots of pots and loading it took a long time.

Nancy paused at the entrance. It resembled the mouth of a cave or the entrance to a shrine. In the dim light, looking back into the belly of the kiln, Nancy saw the arch-roofed chambers stretching back into the hill. As they receded they grew smaller, until the last chamber was almost just a shadowy crawl space. A cool draft wafted out toward Nancy, filling her nostrils with an earthy, smoky smell. Nancy looked around for some kind of door. She recalled Ellie May's talk that morning: wood kilns were generally bricked shut after loading, first by using a large preformed slab to partially seal the entrance, then finishing with individual bricks. There! She saw propped against one side of the opening a large preformed slab of firebricks. Its shape matched the mouth of the kiln, though it was a bit shorter and wouldn't reach more than two-thirds to the top. After that big section was in place, the remaining opening would be sealed with individual bricks and wads of clay.

Nancy poked her head inside the kiln and felt a strange premonition that she wasn't alone. She turned to look over her shoulder, but no one was there. She stood still, held her breath, and listened. The only noises were from the frogs and peepers. Still, the place felt spooky. Nancy forced herself to shake off the feeling. She gathered her courage and stepped inside the first chamber. The roof grazed the top of her head, but she could stand up straight.

The small floodlight on the shed cast a dim light into the mouth of the kiln. At first glance Nancy didn't see any pots. Had Theresa been wrong? Then she flicked on her flashlight and shined it around the chamber. Several large bowls and pots were heaped against one wall of the kiln.

Nancy took a few more steps into the kiln, being careful not to knock against any pots. Sweeping the chamber with her flashlight, she noticed that holes were cut in the sides of the kiln. She remembered these were called stoke holes. When the kiln was fired, the crew would fuel the fire by shoving wood through those holes. Since little light seeped through the holes, Nancy figured they were somehow closed up. Beneath each hole now was a small pile of kindling and straw.

Nancy held her flashlight low to illuminate the pots. Suddenly the light dimmed. Just then she heard a step behind her. Before she could turn, someone punched her in the back, sending her flying. Nancy's head hit something hard. She tried to get up, but her vision began to blur. She heard footsteps, then the sound of something being dragged against the ground, before she passed out.

Nancy came to slowly. Where was she? For a moment she had no idea. She was lying facedown somewhere. The scent in the air was familiar: weenie roast. Nancy felt beneath her hands. Why was the dirt so hard? For a second she had no idea where she was.

Then everything came back to her with a rush. She was inside the anagama kiln. She'd been checking out pots when someone knocked her over from behind. Nancy sat up slowly, fighting back a wave of nausea. The kiln was dark. Something was blocking most of the light from outside. Nancy turned toward the front of the chamber. Someone had blocked the entrance. Rays of light filtered over the top of the door.

Nancy's chest tightened. Get a grip, she told herself. Panic wouldn't help a thing. She told herself firebricks were light. She should be able to open that door. To calm herself, Nancy took a couple of deep breaths and gagged.

Smoke! That cookout smell she had noticed before. Where was it coming from? Nancy struggled to her feet, but as she stood she realized the smoke was thicker toward the ceiling of the kiln. Where was it coming from, she wondered as she dropped back down to her knees. Her hand brushed against something metallic. "My flashlight!"

The sound of her own voice bolstered her courage almost as much as finding the light. Still kneeling, she aimed it at the back chambers of the kiln. The smoke was so thick she could barely make out the flicker of fire.

Horrified, Nancy scrambled to her feet. She staggered backward toward the door, choking and coughing. With every ounce of her strength she threw her weight against the bricks, but the door refused to budge. Nancy redoubled her efforts. The bricks were light. She should have been able to force the door open, but it didn't give.

Nancy's stomach went hollow as she realized what had happened. Whoever had pushed her into the kiln, wedged the door shut to lock her in. They'd started a fire in one of the back stoke holes, then left. Nancy was trapped inside a virtual tinderbox, with no way out.

15

Up in Smoke

Trapped inside a tinderbox! The words roiled in Nancy's head. For a second the thickening smoke seemed to deaden her brain. Then something snapped inside of her.

"No way! I won't give in to this. There's got to be a way out of here!" Nancy muttered through gritted teeth. She kicked at the door, then pounded it with her fists. She raised some brick dust, but the door held fast. She cast a frantic glance back toward the last chamber. The smoke had cleared slightly, but the fire was burning hotter. Flames licked up the kiln walls.

The smoke was collecting toward the front of the kiln, where Nancy stood. Dropping down beneath the curtain of smoke, she looked around, desperate for something to smother the flames. If only she had worn a sweater, she could have used that.

Just then Nancy heard footsteps outside. Someone was nearby.

She heard someone shout, "Caught in the act, Ellie May!" It was Theresa's voice. "I can't believe you'd do this!"

"Do what?" Ellie May sounded nonplussed. "Some idiot started the kiln and—"

"Hey, what's *she* doing here?" Jonathan's voice broke in.

"Jonathan," Ellie May warned, "I'll take care of this."

"Not on your life," Jonathan snarled. "So far your 'taking care of things' has landed us in a real mess. That snoopy Drew person has managed to figure out the whole racket. Not that she'll do much damage now. But I'm getting out while I still can. For all we know she called the cops before you got this harebrained scheme to lock her in the kiln and fire it up."

Ellie May laughed sourly. "No, she thinks I already called them, so she wouldn't bother, I'm sure."

"What about *her*?" Jonathan growled.

"Let me go!" Theresa cried out. "You're hurting me."

"You don't know the first thing about hurt," Jonathan retorted.

"Jonathan, forget about her. We've got to get out of here before someone notices the kiln's lit," Ellie May urged.

Nancy listened in horror from inside the kiln. "Theresa!" she screamed.

"Nancy?" Theresa gasped. "She's in there?"

"She got what was coming to her, spying on us," Jonathan snapped.

"Someone's coming," Ellie May blurted in a panicky voice. "I'm getting out of here now. Leave the girl. There's no time."

Nancy heard some kind of scuffle, then a thud.

"Theresa!" Nancy shouted through the smoky hole, terrified her friend had been dragged away. "Are you there?" Instead of an answer she heard the pounding of running feet—running toward the kiln, not away from it.

"Theresa!" George sounded horrified. "What happened to you?"

"Forget me," Theresa gasped weakly. "I'm okay. It's Nancy. You've got to get her out of that kiln."

"Nancy's in the *kiln?*" Bess's voice was like honey to Nancy's ears.

"Hey, guys," she gasped, coughing through the hole. "Throw in something, anything to help put the fire out."

"There's a hose behind the shed." Theresa shouted, sounding stronger.

"I'll get it," George volunteered.

"Nancy, are you at the door?"

"Yes!" Nancy replied her voice shaking. The temperature was rising, and she was beginning to feel light-headed from lack of air.

"Take this," Theresa commanded, and Nancy felt something wet and heavy dangling from the opening in the door.

Her fingers closed around the damp wool. A field blanket, she realized. It must have been lying around the shed. Theresa had wet it. Nancy struggled toward the back chambers. The fire was sparking in a couple of new bundles of kindling. She beat the blanket against the flames, smothering them as George turned on the hose.

There was a loud crack and pop as water splashed onto the red-hot pots. Dense smoke billowed toward Nancy. She reeled backward and sank down against the door. Why wasn't the door opening? She heard Theresa and Bess grunting, trying to move something.

Theresa was banging something against the door. "I can't do it, Nancy. The bricks are mortared too tight. And they wedged this big rock in to seal it shut. I'm not strong enough to move it."

"But I am." Danny Acero's voice rang clearly through the peep hole. "Nancy's in there?" Nancy heard him ask.

"Danny, hurry." She coughed and gasped. "The fire's out, but the smoke and the heat . . . I . . ."

"Save your breath, Nancy. We'll have you out in no time. Move away from the door."

Nancy heard a loud grunt, then a grating sound. "Pull, guys," Danny commanded. "On the count of three! One. Two. Three." There was the sound of something heavy dropping. Then strong hands reached in the peephole and yanked. The top half of the bricks fell outward, leaving a gaping hole.

Danny reached in and pulled Nancy through the opening. "Good thing you're thin," he said, carrying her away from the kiln. Nancy sank against the shed, gagging and choking. She gulped down lungful after lungful of clean air. For a second she closed her eyes.

Then she remembered. "What happened to Jonathan and Ellie May?" she asked, struggling to her feet.

"They took off in Jonathan's van the minute they saw Danny coming," Theresa said.

"We can't let them get away," Nancy declared.

"What can we do?" Danny sounded disgusted. "Who knows where they're headed?"

"I know exactly where to find them," Nancy said. She turned to Theresa. "Go call the police." Tell them to go to the barn."

Theresa clapped Nancy on the shoulder. "Good thinking. Of course."

Turning to Danny, Nancy asked, "Do you have a car here?"

"No. But I have to tell you that when I got to the pottery studio I caught Michael and David glazing some really interesting pots—duplicates of ones I saw offered in an auction house catalog for some pretty rarefied prices. Michael broke down and told me about Ellie May. He said she came to the studio right after you left tonight, Nancy, and followed you."

Nancy remembered the footsteps behind her on the gravel path. So what she'd heard wasn't just a foraging raccoon. "I'm glad you guessed right, Danny. Now let's get moving. My car's down by the studio, and then it's a good twenty-minute drive to the barn where they've stashed stuff."

"No, it isn't," Theresa said. "Take the river road. Danny, you show her. You know the shortcut."

"Bess, George, stay with Theresa," Nancy told them. "She's been hurt. Make sure someone looks at her arm."

On the ride to the barn, Nancy quizzed Danny. "I don't get it, Danny. Why did you steal Theresa's sketchbook on the day of the fire?"

Danny slouched down in the passenger seat and

let out a dismayed groan. "I'll never live that down, now, will I?"

"The book, Danny," Nancy insisted. "Tell me what that was about."

"As soon as I saw the fire wasn't serious, and the firefighters had it under control, I used it as an excuse to go up to Theresa's room to get the book. I had seen it one day in the library when she was drawing copies of ancient pots from one of the books."

"The book you stole the art plates from!" Nancy surmised, casting a sharp glance at Danny across the seat.

"This is where I'm supposed to grovel with embarrassment, right?" he said with a sheepish grin. "You don't miss a trick, do you, Nancy?" There was great admiration in his voice.

Nancy moistened her lips and tried not to smile. "Why did you need those plates?"

"I wanted to show them to Ellie May. I know it seems like pure idiocy now. Why not show her the book? I wanted to show them to her to compare with the sketchbook. She's expert enough that she could tell me whether she thought that Theresa was involved in the pottery scam."

"Bad move," Nancy remarked.

"Turn here," Danny directed. Nancy made a right off the road and headed up the hill away from the river. "Anyway, I should have realized Ellie May hated Theresa's guts."

"But why? Ellie May's a famous potter, too."

"Famous, yes. But her work is weird. The la-di-das of the ceramic community don't think she's versatile enough to merit the big prizes. Just this year she got passed over for the National Crafts Medal.

"Hey, there's the barn, but I don't see Jonathan's van."

Nancy cut her lights and engine and put her car in neutral. She let it roll silently into a field to the right of the barnyard. "That doesn't mean he's not here."

"You check outside the barn. I'm going in," Nancy said.

Nancy stole around the corner and sidled up to the barn door. Both sides were open. Nancy crept slowly toward the entrance. She could see the flicker of some kind of light or candle playing against the inside wall of the barn. Nancy took a deep breath and stepped inside.

A big blue van had been backed into the barn. Its engine was running and its cargo doors were open. Ellie May was shoving bales of hay into the van. She was working by the light of a kerosene lantern she'd placed on a bale of hay. Nancy took a quick look around. The woman seemed to be alone. Still, Jonathan had to be lurking somewhere.

Ellie May was so intent on her task that she didn't notice Nancy creeping up behind her. "Need help?" Nancy asked sweetly.

Ellie May spun around. "How'd you get—"

"How'd I get out?" Nancy folded her arms across her chest and glared at the woman. "It's a good story. I'll tell you sometime—when I visit you in prison."

Ellie May suddenly peered over Nancy's shoulder. Nancy turned, and Ellie May knocked her to the ground. "I'm not going to jail, or trial, or anything," she fairly spat, and bolted for the van. But Nancy was quicker. She sprang to her feet and tackled Ellie May from behind. As they tumbled to the ground together, Nancy's foot kicked over the lantern. The glass cover fell off, and burning kerosene doused the hay bale. It roared into flames.

Gripping Ellie May's wrist hard, Nancy bounded to her feet and pulled the woman kicking and screaming out of the burning barn. She hauled her clear of the barnyard and into the field. There was a small popping noise, followed by a huge explosion.

"The van!" Ellie May's cry blended with the wail of police sirens.

Nancy pulled Ellie May to her feet and took off the woman's belt. She wrapped it around her wrists and brought her out to the road. They stood silently watching the huge building burn.

"Now, that's pretty dramatic!" Danny said, coming up behind Nancy. He held Jonathan by the collar. "Look what I found trying to hot-wire your car."

"What of it? You can't prove anything!" Jonathan

jerked his head toward the raging fire. "You've got no evidence."

"Oh, but we do. Andrea took samples of just about everything we found in there," Nancy told him. "She stowed it somewhere safe until she could bring it to the cops."

"He was blackmailing me," Ellie May confessed glumly.

"Blackmail?" Nancy was stunned. Out of the corner of her eye she saw the lights of approaching police cars and heard the fire siren ringing back in town. She wanted to find out the whole story before she had to turn Ellie May and Jonathan over to the authorities. "How? And why?"

"Miss Major League Potter here had a pretty good racket going. Thanks to the winters being dead at the Junction, she was able to cook up a whole pile of fake pots for dealers," Jonathan said.

He flashed a nasty grin at Ellie May.

She turned away, tears starting to stream down her cheeks. Nancy felt a moment's pity before she remembered the woman had just tried to roast her alive.

Jonathan continued, "I wanted in. I told her if she didn't connect me to her 'dealers,' then I'd simply call the cops."

"What's happening here?" A state trooper walked up, shoving his hat back on his head.

"A lot!" Nancy exclaimed. "But for starters you'd better arrest these two. They're both forgers."

"And don't forget they tried to murder you," Danny reminded her.

"That, too," Nancy said, then went with the police back to town to fill them in.

16

Danny Owns Up

"The raku firing's supposed to be a high point of your workshop," Danny told Bess, George, and Nancy the next morning as they nursed steaming mugs of coffee outside. "But," he went on with a grin, "I doubt I can match last night's excitement."

"What, not even one exploding barrel?" Bess joked.

"Hey, I wouldn't put down that accident last Sunday," George objected. "If it weren't for you almost getting blown up, we wouldn't have been here. And just think what we would have missed."

"Several attempts on my life for starters!" Nancy said, touching a lump that had formed on her head.

Just then an SUV rolled slowly down the gravel drive in front of the studio past the sleepy students making their way toward the firing. A middle-aged man jumped out. He was wearing chinos, a neat cotton shirt, and a light windbreaker.

He walked right up to Danny.

"Mr. Bye," Danny said, his eyebrows arching. "You weren't supposed to be back until Monday."

"When the police call, you drop everything and come," he said, jiggling his car keys. Danny introduced them all.

Mr. Bye's eyes lighted on Nancy. "So you're the heroine here. I heard all about your adventures from the police this morning. Quite a story. And, off the record, there's more to it." He motioned for the little group to follow him into the studio. "The news will hit the papers soon. But you deserve to hear what's really been happening."

"As it turns out, Jonathan and Ellie May were only pawns in a much bigger, more dangerous game. Interpol's been tracking a ring of art and crafts counterfeiters. They lure artists and artisans into what starts out as a very lucrative business of making fakes. Then they turn the tables and blackmail them into faking masterpieces for very little money. These guys play rough, and there are rumors of some artists going missing—possibly murdered. The police were amazed that the operators had reached out to our

144

community here—though we certainly had the talent on staff."

Mr. Bye left, and the other four went back into the yard.

"Hi, guys, any room for me?" Theresa walked up, lugging a large milk crate full of pots.

"You're going to fire those?" Danny gave a mock look of horror. "Like in raku firing?"

"Like in raku, if you don't mind!" Theresa said. "It's about time you saw what this sweet little refined potter can do when she gets down and dirty!"

Bess looked from Theresa to Danny and nudged Nancy. "She's flirting with him."

"They're flirting with each other," Nancy corrected her, trying not to laugh. "You know how it is on TV in sitcoms. When two people hate each other that much, they're bound to fall in love."

Theresa walked up and handed Nancy a package wrapped in white tissue paper.

"I wanted you to have this as a kind of thank-you, Nancy. You more or less saved my whole career here. Ellie May did a pretty thorough job of framing me."

"I'm just glad she's going where she can do no more harm," Nancy said, accepting the package. She undid the tape, removed the wrapping, and gasped with delight. Theresa had given her one of her large porcelain bowls. Nancy held it up to the sunlight. The porcelain was thin and fine and translucent. "Theresa," she cried, "this is beyond beautiful!"

"And you're beyond wonderful," Theresa said, throwing her arms around Nancy and gathering her in for a hug.

"Since it's time for presents, I have something for you," Danny said. Awkwardly he shoved a large brown paper bag into Theresa's hands. It was tied with twine.

Theresa smiled shyly as she undid the twine. She reached into the brown bag and pulled out a thick black sketchbook. "I had heard you took this!" she cried, and gave Danny a mock glower.

"But wait. Isn't the point that now I'm giving it back?" He cast a pleading glance at Nancy, who threw her hands up and laughed.

"I'm staying out of this," she said.

"Right, only after the mystery's been solved," George teased, guiding Nancy to the place where someone had started the little raku kiln.

The table to the side of the kiln was covered with pots. They ranged from tall elegant vases to Danny's sturdy jugs to Theresa's elegant tea bowls to more awkward pieces from the beginners in the workshop. Nancy spotted one of her bowls instantly. It was chunky, thick rimmed, and not very graceful.

She picked it up and turned to Bess and George. "One thing's for sure," she said, chuckling. "A genuine twenty-first-century Nancy," she said, displaying it to her friends. She met Theresa's eyes and winked as she added, "There's no mystery to who made *this* pot."

American S·I·S·T·E·R·S

Join different sets of sisters as they embark on the varied, sometimes dangerous, always exciting journeys across America's landscape!

West Along the Wagon Road, 1852

A *Titanic* Journey Across the Sea, 1912

Voyage to a Free Land, 1630

Adventure on the Wilderness Road, 1775

Crossing the Colorado Rockies, 1864

Down the Rio Grande, 1829

Horseback on the Boston Post Road, 1704

Exploring the Chicago World's Fair, 1630

by Laurie Lawlor

A MINSTREL® BOOK
Published by Pocket Books

2200-03